THE BOOK OF MARVELS

THE
BOOK
OF
MARVELS

CHRISTOPHER T.
LELAND

CHARLES SCRIBNER'S SONS
NEW YORK

Leland
Chr T.

This is a work of fiction. Names, characters, places, and incidents are either the product of the author's imagination or are used fictitiously. Any resemblance to events or persons, living or dead, is entirely coincidental.

Charles Scribner's Sons
Macmillan Publishing Company
866 Third Avenue
New York, NY 10022
Collier Macmillan Canada, Inc.

Library of Congress
Cataloging-in-Publication Data
Leland, Christopher T.
    The book of marvels / Christopher T. Leland.
    p.   cm.
    ISBN 0–684–19135–0
    I. Title.
PS3562.E4637B6   1989
813'.54—dc20   89–10188   CIP

10 9 8 7 6 5 4 3 2 1

Printed in the United States of America

for Grace

THE BOOK OF MARVELS

O N E

Lila Mae splayed her fingers and waved her hand gently in the air.

"That's a fact, Momma. Hotter than the blue blazes. It is."

She set the heel of her palm on the edge of the table, surveying her nails critically.

"Uh-huh. My land. And on national television! Uh-huh." There was no doubt about it, frost coral was not her color. "No! Well, I never . . ." At least it had been on sale. It was beyond her why she let Mrs. Rudolph down at Mason Hills talk her into things like this. *It'll look so good on you, dear. You have such delicate hands. You should be wearing strong colors.* Well, if she could find the receipt there in the trash can, strongly, without the slightest hint of delicacy, back it was going.

"Why, that is a miracle, Momma, that's for sure. Seventeen years of pain. Can you imagine?"

It sometimes seemed like an utter waste of time, all those hours she spent out at the mall, looking at those cosmetics and pretty clothes, trying to decide what made her look most feminine. Where Wellesley was concerned, she could have worn a gunnysack and there would still be only one thing on his mind. You would have thought they were still in high school.

"Now, now. Momma, you know that Jesus loves you. . . . Sure He does. And I do too. . . . Okay, okay. Bye-bye, now."

Frankly, Lila Mae was not entirely certain Jesus did love Momma. She would certainly understand His reservations. Momma did not make herself all that easy to be wild about. If there were times when she, the woman's own daughter, could cheerfully drop the dear old thing down the nearest well, you really couldn't expect the good Lord, with so many nicer people to concern Himself with, to worry His head too much over the less than pleasant. Then again, she reminded herself, every soul is a special soul, just like they said on "World of Love." Though, of course, they also said that everybody had his cross to bear. Lila Mae suspected that her mother represented hers.

She leaned forward, full into the rush of the fan, and unlaced her tennies. At least, at Quiet Meadows, they didn't require them to wear those ugly white nurse's shoes, which had always reminded her of the ones old ladies and nuns wore, only bleached out, as if to draw greater attention to themselves. Her nurse's-aide uniform really wasn't as awful as she'd imagined it would be. Somehow, that too connected in her imagination with nuns, with those stiff, starched things they wore around their heads, like Debbie Reynolds in that movie, or Sally Field when she was Sister Whatever-her-name, who could fly. Lila Mae had expected some complicated thing of heavy cotton, but, instead, the polyester whites bought secondhand she could rinse out every night and have dry by morning.

She changed into cutoffs and one of the old shirts Eddie'd left behind and she'd never gotten around to throwing out. It didn't smell of him anymore, for which she was grateful. For months, every time she put it on, she'd cry. Not that she wasn't glad he left, she reminded herself again and again. It was just that, in eight years, you do get accustomed to somebody being underfoot, and little things about them: favorite foods and silly things they're afraid of and how they smell. It had been her lucky day that afternoon when she'd walked into the little house over on Allison Street and found all his clothes gone and the note on the kitchen table, taped to it, though she'd always told him not to tape things to the table because it might hurt the finish. It was typical of their entire marriage that, even in leaving, he'd ignored her.

She put some oil in the skillet and set to frying some chicken. It was too hot to cook, really, but this way, she could make enough for cold plates for the next couple of days. The heat was terrifying, especially for this early in the year. Usually, they didn't get temperatures like this till the dog days, but the spring drought had lasted now past Memorial Day, and it looked like there was no relief in sight till autumn.

She checked the clock by the refrigerator. "World of Love" was on at eight, and she wanted to have dinner out of the way, the dishes washed, her uniform ready for tomorrow, and the vacuuming done before it came on. Tonight's guests were that country-and-western singer Abner Halliday, who'd been a drunk and an adulterer for thirty years before he'd found the Lord, praise God, and become a force for good here in these, the Last Days. Him and one of those feminists who had seen the light. It should be an interesting show, and the WOL Singers always put her in a good mood. That little colored girl— LaVonne—was so cute, and the fellow who was the leader looked just like Tommy Lee Henderson back when he was football captain at South Mockdon High, before he went to fat and bought that roadhouse out on Route 9. Lila Mae sighed. So many of the old crowd had ended up bad, one way or another. It was a miracle—an honest-to-goodness one—she'd managed to hold her marriage with Eddie together as long as she had.

That had been no easy chore. She knew within six months of their walk down the aisle it was probably not going to work out, not an easy thing to admit for a good Baptist girl whose own family spoke about divorce in the hushed tones usually reserved for references to sex and other bodily functions. It was not that Eddie was bad to her, particularly. It was simply he wasn't much to her at all. Being married to him did not seem to make things much different than they had been when they were dating. She had thought perhaps fatherhood would settle him down a bit, but that hadn't been in the cards. Indeed, what finally drove Eddie from the house, as nearly as she could figure it, was her suggestion, after two years' worth of tests to make sure her systems were all go where baby-making was concerned, that the problem might be his, and that he ought to make an appointment for a sperm count. She really hadn't thought he would take it so hard, but there again, after eight years, the fact that she couldn't anticipate his reaction indicated just how completely their marriage had failed. Momma still sometimes dinged at her for driving her man away, even after Pastor Allan had spoken to her and suggested that this kind of thing, unfortunate though it might be, happened in the best of families, and assured her that Jesus still loved her, Lila Mae, and Eddie as well, and would continue to through thick and thin.

As she sat there with her chicken and a little of the leftover Rice-a-Roni from last night, the phone rang. She knew it was either Momma again, or Wellesley, who would be home from Midas Muffler by now. Either way, she decided she was in the shower. One session with Momma was enough, at least until after "World of Love," which would give them something to talk about that Lila Mae could contribute to. Momma had a nasty habit of relating programs blow by blow to those who hadn't watched them. Half the time, Lila Mae suspected her mother made up most of it. The problems discussed on the shows always seemed oddly parallel to her own—a poor, sick old lady whose children ignored her; thought her complaints about aches and pains and the dangers of the neighborhood, etc., etc. were all just the silly inventions of a silly old lady, until, one fine day . . .

Well, Momma could stew till nine o'clock, and Wellesley could stew forever. There were certain things Lila Mae just could not forgive, and he'd certainly earned her undying contempt and then some. It was bad enough that, on their fifth date, mind you, he had propositioned her. But he'd also had the gall, before he realized she was speechless not because she was pleased but because she was furious, to ask if she had any of . . . of those little things that men put on. The very idea! As if she would tote a pack around in her purse like a roll of Life Savers!

When he figured out she was offended, which took so long

Lila Mae concluded he was not only dirty-minded but dense, he fell all over himself to make amends, and had been doing so ever since. He had called her time after time at home, heedless of her hanging up, till she finally stopped answering the phone; then he had tried to get her at work, to the point she told Edna at the front desk to screen her calls. There had been two "Thinking of you" cards, and a bouquet of flowers on her doorstep from "An admirerror," who had to be Welles-ley, who had had serious problems, Lila Mae recalled having heard, learning to spell his own name. Lila Mae thought that in an odd way that particular misspelling might have some sort of larger significance. She had become interested in deciphering various kinds of messages from the Bible-study classes she tuned in to some nights before she went to bed, when all kinds of things were explained which otherwise didn't make sense in Scripture. In that signature, though probably he wasn't even aware of it, Wellesley had admitted that he "admires error." The *es* was missing, of course, but she had gathered from the programs that such minor details really weren't im-portant. It was as if a Divine hand had guided his pen, so as to warn her that, though she might be tempted, Wellesley was as good as the snake in the Garden where she was concerned.

There was some truth to that, for she had liked Wellesley Coe ever since she was a little girl. He was three years older than she was, and had always been a thoughtful and soft-spoken boy, not a sissy, but one of the ones who did not mind having to baby-sit now and then and who could be trusted to give you the correct change when you had him run errands. When he mowed the yard, he took pride in a job well done and didn't ignore the clumps of grass under the bushes or along the fence like Lila Mae's brothers did. He had sandy hair that he had slicked back with tonic ever since he was a boy and the greenest eyes she had ever seen on anybody, man or woman, and they just seemed to get greener and greener as he grew up. Since the divorce, she had gone out with a few men she had known from church, but, frankly, they had been a little dull, bumbling or too serious or awfully stuck on themselves. So, when Wellesley, who was raised a Methodist, but really wasn't a practicant of much of anything, asked her out, she was willing to grant him a little extra space in exchange for a stronger touch of romance.

He hadn't disappointed her. The good-night kiss after their first movie had sent a chill right through her, and the way he always brought her a little something when he took her out, the way he held her hand and looked deep in her eyes when he gave the present to her, the way he'd kiss her right along the hairline when she, giggling, took the box from him: all those things really made her believe that, perhaps, there was a future with him.

It was too bad he had proved himself unworthy.

She rinsed off the dishes and put the skillet to soak, then puttered about picking up. She considered turning on the news or "Wheel of Fortune," but the former was too depressing and she had heard on some program that the wheel was connected somehow with the Black Mass and Satan worship, so perhaps it was best to leave Pat Sajak and Vanna White to pave their own way to Hell. Certainly there were enough nefarious influences down at Quiet Meadows without exposing her soul to any that came over the airways. When she started the job, she really was taken aback a bit at the—what was the word?—well, the caliber of people she was working with. Quiet Meadows, after all, was owned by a Baptist organization, or, at least, that was her understanding, which meant no liquor for the patients, no dancing (though that frankly was not too much of a hardship for most of them), no card-playing (which was, at least for some), and daily prayer services after lunch. The patients were not allowed cigarettes, though the staff was, and at times the lounge resembled some anteroom of the Other Place. Lila Mae had expected her coworkers to be quiet, sober, serious folk, good Christian people, as her mother would say. She was willing to be relatively liberal in her definitions, mind you, but still, she anticipated something far different from the congregation of crackpots and heathens she had found.

Then again, perhaps that wasn't quite fair. It wasn't as if Lila Mae knew a great deal about this kind of work, having, in those years she was married to Eddie, spent most of her time as a housewife, with an occasional seasonal stint at Delaney's at Mason Hills during the Christmas rush. It was not that she did not want to work. It was that Eddie did not want her to. On that, he was adamant: "No wife of mine . . ." and "I can provide what . . ." and even, in a rare moment of religiosity for him, "It says that the man shall live by the sweat of his brow, not the woman." The sentiments were nice, even if the consequences of them were largely boredom and too much time spent talking to Momma on the phone. For a while, her church work at Third Baptist gave Lila Mae some outlet, but she discovered that being around those who seemed to have made loving Jesus a career could make loving Him for the heck of it more difficult than she suspected He intended, and she had gradually drifted out of the congregation.

After the separation, she had used the money in the joint bank account to get by, and her brother Fred had loaned her a thousand dollars on the sly so Momma wouldn't know. But she'd realized from the first she'd have to get a job, and after a couple of unsuccessful investigations of retail and secretarial work, she'd ended up at Quiet Meadows pretty much by default. She herself had never had to face the burdens of caring for the sick: Momma, for all her hypochondria, had the constitution of a dray horse, and Daddy had simply fallen over dead of a heart attack after forty years of never missing a day of work due to illness. Her brothers had all been healthy boys; she had no children to nurse through measles, mumps, the croup, and so on. But she discovered that there remained the firm conviction in the mind of America, or, at least, in that portion of it which resided in the personnel office of Quiet Meadows, that all women by their very nature knew how to take care of people in need. She wasn't sure she agreed with that, but, given how desperate she was for work by the time she interviewed with them, she made no effort to disabuse them.

She snapped on "World of Love" just as the phone began to jangle again. She should have unplugged it, but was hesitant to now until it stopped ringing. She had a sneaking suspicion that, somehow, the person on the other end of the line could hear you drawing the cord out of the jack. Whoever it was was persistent, and she completely missed the theme music, which had an upbeat, contemporary sound, sort of like a Burt Bacharach song. Finally, the ringing stopped, and she settled in for the confessions of Abner Halliday.

At nine o'clock on the dot, the phone started up again, with Lila Mae softly weeping there in the La-Z-Boy. It had been a very moving testimony, and Halliday had indeed been a thoroughly bad man before he found the Lord. At other, less emotional moments, Lila Mae sometimes wondered if it were quite fair that truly spectacular sinners had no more difficult access to salvation than those who had generally lived dull little lives with an occasional attack of avarice over a neighbor's new car or a little lust in their hearts for some cute guy on the afternoon soaps. But such notions did not occur to her as she thought just how far down the primrose path Abner Halliday had wandered: liquor and drugs and Mafia friends and fast girls and even fast boys before he had finally seen the light, thank the Lord, and set his eyes on Jesus. If she had not been so distraught, she wouldn't have picked up the receiver, but she was so beside herself she forgot just who the likely candidates at the other end of the line might be.

"Hello," she sniffled.

It was her mother.

"No, no. Momma. No, it was just 'World of Love' . . . Uh-huh. Abner Halliday. That was the most moving testimony. . . . No, no I didn't get to see it tonight. . . . Well, I don't see how it could have been even more inspirational. . . ."

Lila Mae Bower had accepted Jesus Christ as her personal savior and so been born again at the age of thirteen. It was quite the thing to do at the time, and a number of her friends had been in line with her for baptism by immersion at the pool at Third Baptist. All had been in the midst of that peculiar metaphysical period that accompanies puberty in both boys and girls, a last stand of childhood against the rampaging hormones that are in the process of transforming the innocent into walking opportunities of sin. Lila Mae differed from her friends, however, in that she had always had a certain religious bent. In the first and second grades, she found that the nuns attached to St. Anne's School up in Mockdon exercised a peculiar fascination for her, darkly garbed even on the hottest summer days, robed too with a special mystery, a communal and sacrificial faith that offered, in Lila Mae's mind, a security that the Baptist Church, with its focus on each individual's redemption, could not provide.

A dose of antipopish propaganda at Sunday school and from Momma cured her of her Catholic sympathies, though not of her longings for a church more distinctive and magical than the Baptist. There was little unique about being a Baptist in Rhymers Creek. It seemed every other friend she had at school she saw again on Sunday. In the sixth grade, she did a complicated project on the Amish, and imagined moving to Pennsylvania Dutch country and taking up life as a plain person, dressing in long gingham dresses and sunbonnets and looking for all the world as if she had just stepped out of one of those early-life-on-the-frontier movies they showed sometimes in social studies. The discovery that the Amish did not actively proselytize, that, indeed, they discouraged if not downright forbade converts, shattered her for a day or two, as she saw her dreams of the simple life go up in smoke. For a while, she entertained notions of running away to Bethlehem or Lancaster and so impressing the Amish with her convictions that they would welcome her into the fold, but she finally decided it would simply be too much of a gamble and she would probably miss everybody and there was no way she could get the money for a bus ticket anyway. She would just have to settle for the conventions of the Baptist Church and get on with it.

So, when she was baptized, Lila Mae really did mean it, in a mature way different from her friends. If this was the best the Lord could do for her in Rhymers Creek, or she, for Him, then she would certainly have a crack at it. She was a little scandalized, growing older, at the girls who did nothing all week but covet their neighbors' goods—clothes, shoes, makeup, hand-bags, boyfriends—and then showed up at services on Sundays (dressed to the nines, of course) as if they were the humblest, most demure, and least concerned-about-worldly-pleasures girls in the county. Later on, the occasional comments she over-heard regarding the sexual escapades of boys in her class and particularly the girls shocked her even more, some of them the very same individuals who had stood with her, soaked and saved, so very few years before.

The paradoxes of faith remained with her as she became an adult, the desire to be a good Christian before the temptations of the world at the same time that that world was changing at a remarkable pace, as was her own place in it. Her gradual falling away from Third Baptist had less to do with her feelings about God and Jesus in her soul than her feelings about the sniping, back-stabbing, conspicuous consumption, and all-around nas-tiness beneath a mask of smiles and good fellowship that characterized the congregation. The more solitary worship the Spiritual Broadcasting Company offered when it arrived in Mockdon County not that long before the end of her marriage provided, oddly, a kind of personal solace that Third Baptist failed to offer. Miracles were happening everywhere. Life was happy and good even in the Last Days, and the faithful had only better things to look forward to. Even amid the horrors of Armageddon, according to some of the preachers, the pure of heart would be raptured up to God and so miss the truly hellish conditions that would mark the time before the final battle.

So, she had stopped going to church altogether, except on the occasional holiday or some other special occasion: a wed-ding, a baptism or funeral. Certain people looked askance at this change, including her brother Lonnie and his wife, Betsy, who, while not very devout, saw definite social advantages in being seen lustily bellowing "Onward, Christian Soldiers" or "Revive Us Again" in the fourth row of the starkly modern new sanctuary, which Lila Mae had always thought looked more like a bank than a church. For her, however, the flickering images of Ted and Becky Standish offered a better way of dealing with the odd dislocation she felt in the midst of a world she had always known which sometimes seemed to her as different, though in no way as attractive, as that land of plain people far to the east where she had once dreamed of beginning her life anew.

She had just pulled into her parking spot when Eliot showed up on his bike. Eliot was immense, at least six six, she estimated, and his bike was even bigger. It roared like an Indy car on two wheels, all chrome and shiny black paint with tongues of flame painted on the gas tank, looking, Lila Mae imagined, like the kind of vehicle Satan might affect when making his earthly rounds. And Eliot, unfortunately, with his tattoos, his earring (which he continued to wear despite protests from both patients and Mrs. Lindley, the administrator), his jacket straight out of one of those old Peter Fonda movies, and gruff and often unspeakably foulmouthed way of talking, was likely the physical semblance the Devil would find appropriate as well. To make matters worse, she had discovered, not long after she started work, he was queer as a three-dollar bill.

"Howdy, Lila Mae," he growled as he swung himself off the demon machine and pulled his tennies out of the compartment in back. "How's tricks?"

Lila Mae flinched. "Good morning, Eliot. How are you this morning?"

"Same old shit. You know, Lile."

In addition to everything else, Eliot had the annoying habit of shortening everybody's name into something it wasn't. Even Mrs. Lindley became "Miz Lind" for him.

"Well, is that a fact," she said neutrally, as she turned, noting, as she often did, the contrast between Eliot's immense bike and her little gray Ford with its "Honk If You Love Jesus" bumper sticker. She made a beeline for the door.

Inside, even at 6:30 A.M., the air-conditioning felt good. The night crew was finishing charts, and Nurse Phillips was conferencing with Nurse Palmer so the chain of medical knowledge might remain unbroken. Lila Mae went to the lounge for a cup of coffee before she started her rounds. Priscilla and Billie Jean were already there, while Lee, the other orderly, was probably trying to make time with Consuela, the Mexican cook they had hired last week. She spoke very little English, as near as Lila Mae could make out, and had yet to learn that Lee was a snake in the grass who would say or do anything to get a woman into his bed. Norma would be late, as usual, probably teary as the result of some new heartbreak. Lila Mae had never known anyone whose life was so unspeakably and uninterruptedly awful—except perhaps for Momma—which led her to suspect that many of Norma's crises were at the least exaggerations, if not downright falsehoods.

She heard Eliot pass behind her, stow his lunch in the refrigerator, and then rumble by again, off in search of Stewart, the night orderly, also "that way," with whom he shared whatever gossip people like that shared, she supposed. Stewart was a lithe, immaculate man, the color of those Nestlé bars Lila Mae loved, as graceful as Eliot was lumbering. She slouched down into the chair beside Priscilla.

"So, how does the day look?"

"If Norma's not too late, things should be pretty smooth," Billie Jean said. "I guess Mrs. Limerick was transferred to St. Justin's about three o'clock this morning, and Mrs. Samuels finally checked out on the swing shift."

Lila Mae sighed. "Well, I hate to say it, but it's kind of a blessing. . . ."

"Oh, you don't hate to say it," Priscilla said snippily. "You love to say it. You say it every time somebody checks out."

Lila Mae bristled. After all, she had only started here three weeks before.

"Can it, Priscilla," Billie Jean said. "You know Lila Mae's right. With those bedsores she had. After how long in there not even knowing who the hell she was. Nine-tenths of the time, it is a blessing when they go."

Priscilla tossed her tinted, feathered hair, stood, and flounced out of the room without a word.

"Well," Lila Mae sniffed. "What's she so cranky about?"

"Probably on the rag, honey," Billy Jean said, taking a long draw on her Salem, her gray eyes still lazy in the fluorescent glare of the lounge. "It always comes around the fourteenth."

Billie Jean had a fabulous memory, a true gift, Lila Mae thought. With all her patients, she could ask after children, grandchildren, cousins, all their doctors by name. She remembered birthdays and deathdays as well. Doubtless, in six months, when someone said, "When was it Samuels checked out?" Billie Jean would mutter the correct month and date, together with the fact that Priscilla had been having her period that day.

Billie Jean snuffed her cigarette as Stewart and Eliot rolled into the room, both convulsed in giggles.

". . . a cold day in the Cowboy's locker room before that one gets anything off of him!"

Eliot shrugged. "That's the story. And with the piece he packs . . ."

Lila Mae raised her eyes to Heaven.

"Come on, boys and girls." Billie Jean stood and stretched. "Time to set up the exhibits."

Breakfast went relatively smoothly. Norma made it in by quarter of seven, severely depressed but functional, and draw-sheets were changed and catheter bags emptied before the trays came out. Lila Mae had Run Three, which L'ed around the south hall and the back corridor. They all referred to it as Skid Row. It tended to be quiet. A point in favor of the comatose was that they neither complained nor made demands, and the percentage of the living dead on Skid Row was higher than on either The Gutter or Tin Pan Alley, or on either of the men's runs: Flaccid Farms and Wheelieville. She was ahead of herself with the bedmaking and patient-turning at ten when Norma appeared at the door of Mrs. Perkins' and Miss Johnson's room, looking distraught.

"Lila, Lila, come quick! Lee's ruptured himself again, I think. Oh, come quick! Come quick!"

Hustling down the hall after Norma, she wondered why on earth she had come to get her, rather than Nurse Palmer. She was a sweet girl but she really didn't have a brain in her head. By the time they arrived, Nurse Palmer was there anyway, likely alerted by Lee's outrageous moaning. He was doubled over against the empty bed in Mr. Schroeder's room, bellowing piteously, with his arms crossed over his middle. Mr. Schroeder, immensely fat, gazed on goggle-eyed and mute as Nurse Palmer shoved Lee down on the bed and unbuckled his pants. By this time Eliot was there as well.

"Schroeder, you barrel of lard, what the hell have you done now?" he roared.

"Shut up, Eliot!" Nurse Palmer snapped. "Stretch out, Lee. All right. All right." She straightened him out and efficiently shooshed down his Jockey shorts. Lila let out a little "Eek" and turned her head.

"Oh, come on, Lila Mae," Eliot said, "it's not that big."

Nurse Palmer probed around a bit, blocking the view of the rest of the staff with her body. "You're okay, Lee," she said. "It's probably just a groin pull. But you better get on over to emergency and see Dr. Boone just in case." She turned to the others. "Back to work, everybody. Eliot, get Mr. Schroeder out of bed."

"Show's over, girls." Eliot shooed Norma and Lila Mae toward the door. "And it wasn't really that supercolossal ballpark frank we'd been expecting, was it?"

"Eliot, you . . ." Lila began.

Norma burst into tears and ran up the hall.

"What's with her?" Eliot asked.

"I don't know," Lila Mae sighed. "You know Norma."

"Who has three today?" Nurse Palmer had helped Lee over to the chair in the corner.

"I do."

"Eliot, go get him one of the wheelchairs and have Edna call a cab, then get back here and take care of Schroeder. Lila Mae, you'll split five with Eliot today. Lee's got over half of them up. You'll just need to do the beds and check the bath list."

"Yes, ma'am."

On her way back to her own run, Lila Mae prayed for

patience. She had a terrible suspicion, which was probably totally unfair, that Lee had arranged some tryst or other for this afternoon, and that's why he had suffered the accident lifting Mr. Schroeder. Billie Jean got the fat old thing up by herself, and she was a good foot shorter and thirty pounds lighter than Lee was. A double run was always a nightmare, and she hated doing the men anyway. She knew she shouldn't be embarrassed, just as Nurse Palmer wasn't with Lee. A patient is a patient, and you can't let silly notions of modesty get in the way of helping other people out. But the only man she had ever really seen naked before she came to work here had been Eddie, and even then she always felt a little uncomfortable when he wanted to make love in broad daylight or with all the lights on. He'd once tried to convince her to do it outside, when they'd gone on a picnic near the Willowood Reservoir, but she'd put her foot down on that one. Still and all, they had ended up at a motel on the way home.

By lunchtime, she had pretty well managed to finish Skid Row, though every time she passed the nurses' station, it seemed like the page board there was lit up like the control panel in one of those nuclear-disaster movies, where everything has gone haywire and a deafening siren is going WHOOP! WHOOP! WHOOP! in the background. All the men on five wanted to be out of bed, whirring on their way in their wheelchairs or hobbling along on their canes, out and about, doing what had to be done. Good Lord, what did they have to hurry about anyway? She would break off the work on three from time to time to try to see if there were any real emergencies that needed taking care of. Aside from a bathroom visit for Mr. Pope, there really weren't, and she gave Mr. Gumbal quite a talking to for ringing twice to ask her just when precisely she planned to get him up and dressed. She did notice that both Billie Jean and Eliot were answering her pages from time to time, for which she silently blessed their hearts. If only Norma would pick up a few, she might actually get ahead of the game. She had no such illusions where Priscilla was concerned.

Keeping her sanity, or a semblance thereof, in the midst of it all required a good deal of Lila Mae's Christian forbearance. Mrs. Perkins had been a terror to dress this morning for some reason, refusing to stay in anything put on her. It seemed every ten minutes she was wandering the halls topless again, and Lila Mae would have to corral her and get her into a blouse. Ellie Breckenridge, meanwhile, was in one of her manic moods, hectoring every patient she could roll up to to come to the picnic she was planning at some park in Galveston, where, as near as Lila Mae could determine, she had lived sometime around 1936.

"We'll have cold chicken and potato salad, and I want you to bring a dessert. Can you make a pecan pie? I'm doing my ham, of course. . . ."

By two, amidst much whining and complaining, she had gotten all the men underway. It was not quite so difficult as she had feared it would be. There was so much to be done she really didn't think too much about having to see and sometimes adjust in their Jockeys that shriveled equipment between their legs. And she had to admit, despite it all, the men really did tend to be a tad more tolerant, a little more understanding, than the ladies were. Some of them were so cute: Mr. Meachum, who had had a stroke and couldn't talk, but whistled, like a parrot, gesturing with his one good arm for yes or no; his roommate, Mr. Ricks, who was very polite to her and asked her how her day was going and was sympathetic when she told him not too well; and Billy McNeely, who had been there forever and was slightly retarded, and always asked whoever was on the run if it might be possible to sneak him a deck of cards for solitaire. Still, by the time she was done, she was exhausted, and there was a good hour to go before charting time, which meant Nurse Palmer would want her to see who was on the bath list.

The shower girls came on Tuesdays and Thursdays, and it really was their job to make sure everybody was clean. But, inevitably, they would fall behind or somebody would be too weak to get up or have a cold or visitors or a doctor on the way, so the aides would have to pick up any slack where bathing was concerned. Mrs. Voxburg on Skid Row needed to be taken care of, though of the men, there was only Mr. Ricks, who should be no trouble. If she hurried, she'd still get her charting done and be able to punch out by three.

Beside the bed with a basin of warm, soapy water, a fresh gown for Mrs. Voxburg on the chair beside her, and Mrs. Voxburg herself—staring into space, with that whimpering, as-tonished look of a chick recently hatched—naked on the sheets, Lila Mae felt, as she often did when giving sponge baths, a little like Jesus. The experience always made her think of Jesus washing the feet of the disciples. Was that sacrilegious? Maybe it would be better to imagine herself Mary of Bethany, drying the feet of the Master with her hair. She harrumphed: that was certainly the Biblical scene Wellesley Coe would have preferred.

It made her so angry, the way he had treated her, the as-sumption he made that of course she would want to go to bed with him, without so much as real time to get to know each other, much less a wedding ring. Not even any declaration of intentions. She knew that's how things were supposed to work in the modern world, not just in Hollywood, but right here in Rhymers Creek, but she had worked hard all her life to be a respectable girl and after that a respectable woman. Even if it seemed old-fashioned, she still thought reputation counted for something. You could never be sure when times might change again and you'd be called on the carpet for those things you did because everybody was doing them. Wellesley, along with a lot of other people, probably thought that she would be a gay divorcée—in that old sense of the term, which meant she was loose, not that she was looking for another lady—and it was not, despite her reservations about doing it outdoors, that she had anything against sex. She had read *Total Woman*, and though she couldn't quite picture herself in leopardskin panties and refused to do over the bedroom so it looked like a Turkish whorehouse, she had never felt she failed Eddie in that department. She'd very much enjoyed that department herself, thank you. It wasn't any sexual coolness on her part that had wrecked her marriage.

She passed the washrag firmly down Mrs. Voxburg's arm. The old woman moaned softly, but her eyes remained fixed on the ceiling, her expression unchanged. Beneath the cloth, her skin flaked away in small, fine pieces, like the chips off a sheet of mica. Lila Mae remembered her grandfather showing her that once, when she couldn't have been more than four, scraping what he called isinglass with his fingernail, the shiny surface flaking off bits of itself clear as diamonds. Mrs. Voxburg's skin, though, was cloudy, like her eyes, like whatever remained inside that white-headed skull of hers.

Lila Mae continued on to the gnarled fingers, bent with arthritis, the nails thick and discolored. They brought a manicurist in only once a month, with the hairdresser, and there were far too many patients for them to see in a single day. She would have to find the clippers to shear these talons off. She felt that humid sadness begin to steal through her, the one she had to guard against, the one she knew she would suffer from when she took this job. She had anticipated it because of Momma, looking at that woman she remembered as vigorous and seeing her instead as crabbed, unkempt, unhappy. Still, Momma had no notion of how lucky she was. It seemed a terrible fate for God to arrange for everyone: to shrivel and wrinkle, shorten and spot. At the least, even if their strength and memory weren't what they once were, people should have the dignity of being beautiful when they got old. It wasn't that they all had to look like they were seventeen, like some model in Glamour. Just whole, complete, bright-eyed and straight-limbed. If God hadn't taken care of it, she thought as she stroked that soft turkey throat, at the least, people could help out. The hairdresser and manicurist should come every day. They could spend eight hours making all these old people as beautiful as they could be: makeup, wigs, pretty dresses, permanents, manicures and pedicures, dye jobs, flowers and bows.

She pulled away the sheet she had used to cover Mrs. Voxburg's private place, wrung out the washrag, and began, delicately, to wash her shoulders, her shrunken breasts and belly. Gravity had done a job there, she noted ruefully. Gravity and how many babies?

She caught her breath. That sadness exploded all through her. That was the sorriest part of all. If only she and Eddie could have had that baby they both wanted so bad, maybe things would have worked out. Maybe fatherhood would have made him grow up, put away childish things, like Saint Paul said, and pay attention to what a grown man was supposed to pay attention to.

But probably not. Eddie was going to be nothing but an overgrown boy all his life, and who knew that Mr. Voxburg hadn't been the same way, that Mrs. Voxburg had dreamed from time to time of cutting him loose and making a new start before the babies came and it was too late? Had she imagined a Wellesley Coe? Some dream man, a little more mature, a little more romantic. Or had him for real, sneaking out from time to time to meet him? And had he ruined it all by asking her during one of those secret rendezvous if she had any of those little things that men put on?

She shook her head disgustedly, and moved her hand down toward Mrs. Voxburg's stomach. She stroked it easily back and forth over the wrinkled skin, almost painfully gentle. A sweet blankness settled over her. Mrs. Voxburg began to moan, a slow keening sound, halfway between a coo and a cry.

Hush, little baby, don't say a word,
Papa's gonna buy you a mockingbird.
If that mockingbird don't sing,
Papa's gonna buy you a diamond . . .

Lila Mae stopped in mid-stanza. What was she doing? She let forth a little gasp, and hurriedly finished washing Mrs. Voxburg, a funny tightness in her throat. She had to stop with this silliness. Here she was mothering a lady old enough to be her own mother, maybe even her grandmother! It was ridiculous.

She poured the water out in the sink in the bathroom, then went back and got Mrs. Voxburg into her gown. She took some clean sheets off her cart and remade the bed underneath the old woman, a skill she had become expert at in these few weeks. She flashed down the corridor on her way to Mr. Ricks's room, checking the page board as she passed and nearly colliding with Priscilla, her arms piled with linens, as if she were just starting her run.

"What's happened?"

Priscilla snorted. "Disaster in The Gutter. Five wet beds. I don't know why I stay at this place." Then she was gone. Lila Mae felt a certain contented amusement.

There was a light for Number 35. She stopped in on her way to Mr. Ricks's room. It was Mrs. Wallerby, or, rather, Mrs. Wallerby's two boys, Elmer and Heck. They both turned and smiled at her idiotically as she crossed the threshold.

"Oh, hello," Elmer said. "We just noticed that Mother's ice-water pitcher was empty. Do you think you could fill it up?"

Lila Mae looked at him murderously. Both he and his brother were fat as sin and never lifted a finger when they came on a visit. Beyond that, they had a gruesome way of preening whenever they were around, like crows over a carcass. "Sure."

"ISN'T THAT NICE, MOTHER!!" Elmer shouted. "SHE'S GETTING YOU SOME ICE WATER."

The boys had convinced themselves some time ago their mother was stone deaf, though as nearly as Lila Mae could determine, the old lady heard about as well as anybody else at eighty-five. She had developed a notable stammer, which both her sons and the doctors attributed to a slight stroke, though Eliot confided in Lila Mae the first day that he thought it was the result of having her two hulking, blubberous sons bellowing at her all the time.

She brought the pitcher back from the cooler.

"Thank you so much," Elmer said unctuously, and Heck, whom Lila Mae had rarely heard utter a sound, nodded, if it were possible, in an equally oily way. Beating her retreat, she felt oddly greasy, as if she had just stepped back from the griddle at McDonald's.

When she rattled the plastic shower chair into Mr. Ricks's room, he was in his bathrobe, sitting in the armchair by the bed, reading the newspaper. Mr. Meachum, standing by the window, whistled a greeting to her, and gestured wildly for her to come over to his side.

"Hi there, hi there!" she said, struggling to maneuver the casters over the indoor/outdoor carpeting. "Time for your shower, Mr. Ricks."

He turned to her. He was not as old as most of the patients here, or didn't seem so, somewhere probably in his seventies. He had a large, handsome head, like that, she thought, of a heroic statue she had seen in a book someplace. His hair was thin in front, but he still had a certain sparkle in his eyes. She wondered what his problem was.

"What a nice surprise," he said. "I thought since they'd forgotten me yesterday I'd have to wait for a few more days."

"Well, here I am," Lila said with forced cheer. "Just climb aboard and we'll take care of you."

Throughout it all, Mr. Meachum had continued to beckon and whistle with ever-increasing insistence.

"Not right now, honey." Lila Mae had gotten the thing situated so she could plant Mr. Ricks on it. "I don't have time for any window gazing right now."

The shower chair was, for Lila Mae, one of the most humiliating contraptions she had ever seen. It was efficient, surely; that was the reason for its design. But there was something grotesque about it, all blown turquoise plastic with a hole in the seat, like a giant potty chair. When the shower girls used it, they took no precautions, and she would see patients wrapped in towels being spun down the hallways, their bare shrunken bottoms flapping through the hole underneath. As always, she had put a towel across it, and as she helped Mr. Ricks settle in, she assured herself it was in place. She straightened his robe before she threw the bath towel across him. The whole effect was almost Roman, like one of those pictures in the illustrated New Testament. Mr. Ricks sat very straight in the chair, and the towel fell across him in dipping folds. On the way down the hall he looked friendly but serious, and waved discreetly now and then to a few of the ladies.

When they got to the shower, she tried not to hurry, though she knew it was already close to quitting time, and she couldn't leave till she got her charting done.

"How do you like the water, Mr. Ricks?"

"Good and hot, dear. Opens up the pores."

Quiet Meadows' showers were incapable of anything more than mildly tepid temperatures, but Lila Mae did the best she could. The tiled room was always chilly, which meant even the hint of warmth produced considerable steam. After she had adjusted the water, she pulled the towel off Mr. Ricks, and he extended his arms so she could remove his robe. It was then she noticed the scar, like an angry welt down his hip. Still, it struck her, as she wheeled him into the spray, how Mr. Ricks maintained an odd dignity even in the nude. His body had all the sags and bags and liver spots the other patients had, along with that peculiar smell that can only be described as old. And yet he had a kind of gravity in the set of his flesh, in the way he held his head, that elicited not pity, certainly not desire, but a peculiar respect.

"You're new, dear, aren't you?" he said as she scrubbed his back.

"Why, yes. Yes, I am. I started about three weeks ago."

"I didn't think I'd seen you. Could you get that place there down at the base of my ribs? It's been itching something awful. I'm pretty new here myself, but I try to keep track of who's who."

"Well," Lila Mae said, pushing him forward slightly in search of that elusive spot, "people do come and go here pretty frequently, I imagine."

"Some more permanently than others." Mr. Ricks chuckled.

Lila didn't know quite how to react. The staff survived on gallows humor, but the patients rarely talked about death outright, though, as she thought of it now, there was an odd allusiveness in remarks made now and then. She allowed herself to chuckle too.

"Well, it doesn't look to me like you're going to be going anywhere but home from here."

He shrugged as she moved to his chest. "Hard to know on that one, dear. What is your name?" He squinted at her name tag. "Lila Mae," he read. "It's hard to know, Lila Mae. But I'll take what comes."

"No apologies and no regrets," she said cheerily.

"Oh, no. Of those I've got a million," he said with real heartiness. "But there's no use crying over spilled milk, after all."

"That's a fact," she said, planting the shower head in its keeper and shifting it away as she knelt down to clean his feet, "You always have to be looking toward the future. Any one of us could meet his Maker at any time."

"Well, if He's up there, I've got a long list of things to take up with Him."

"Why, Mr. Ricks," she said from down between his toes, "whatever does that mean?"

"Oh, I don't know. Cancer, for example," he said. "I just can't quite figure out why He'd loose something that awful on so many of us."

"Now," she said soothingly, remembering what they would say on "World of Love," "you have to think of disease as a thing of Satan, that's all. It's not God's fault."

"I don't know, Lila Mae. Satan's got to be God's fault, then, so it does come down to His responsibility."

Lila Mae didn't reply, suddenly finding a stubborn spot on Mr. Ricks's calf that, though she knew it wasn't dirt, she nonetheless pretended might be. These kinds of larger theological questions never appealed to her. They always seemed to veer dangerously close to the sort of doubt and unbelief they warned about on the Christian broadcasts, the kind of thing the proabortion secular humanists were always bringing up. It just seemed much simpler to place all the blame with the Devil and leave it at that.

"Well," she said to break the silence, "God works in mysterious ways, I guess."

"Or He has one hell of a sick sense of humor." Mr. Ricks grunted as she went after his face with the washrag.

"Shame on you!" she sniffed, though she seriously was half-scandalized. It wasn't the kind of talk she quite expected from an old man.

"Now I've done it." He smacked the seat of the chair with one hand. "Now I've riled you."

"You did no such thing," she said quickly, grabbing the shower head to rinse him.

She sprayed the soap off, and spattered herself a good deal in the process. The conversation had unnerved her somehow. She reached for the towel.

"Lila Mae," he said, "I know it's none too pleasant for a pretty thing like you, especially with an old geezer like me, but I was always very careful about my hygiene down there. . . ."

She stiffened. "I didn't mean to overlook anything," she said stiffly, soaping up the washrag again and steeling herself to do her duty.

She wheeled Mr. Ricks back into his room at three on the dot. Mr. Meachum was still by the window, watching the world go by. He glanced at them morosely as they came through the door, as if he begrudged Lila Mae's lack of attentiveness earlier.

As she helped him back into the armchair, Mr. Ricks said, "Now, honey, you're not mad at me about what I said in there?"

"Don't be silly, Mr. Ricks." She took the blanket off the bed and settled it over his knees. "I guess I just hadn't thought about some things quite that way."

"Well, you come by now and then and we'll talk some more," he said, and then winked at her. "I think we've got a lot to say to each other."

"I suppose we do." She bustled toward the door. She couldn't understand what it was about him that made her so uncomfortable, but with her charting still to do, she wasn't going to take the time to think about it.

She had just sat down at the nurses' station when Priscilla passed by on her way out.

"Lila Mae, that little Ford, the sort of mousy gray one, that's yours, isn't it?"

"Yes."

"So who's your secret admirer?"

"What?"

Priscilla was down the hall. "Ask Frank Meachum. He saw it all."

Whatever could she be talking about? Lila Mae sat for an instant, then set down the chart. She hustled down the hall and out the front door. The heat hit her like a blackjack, but still she broke into a run. Eliot was putting on his helmet as she arrived, getting ready to mount his bike. Her car was next to him, unscathed. On the back window, however, in brilliant green shaving cream now melting in the sun, it said in bold letters:

"I ♥ LILA MAE/WC."

"Oh!"

Her hands went to her face. How could he! She scrambled through her pockets, but she had nothing to clean the mess off with. She stood there, stiff with rage and already sticky with sweat.

"Gee," Eliot said, motioning first to the back window, then to the bumper sticker, "and you think I'm weird, Lile. Jesus and bathrooms?"

His foot slammed down as he kick-started the bike, and he roared away. She stood in the cloud of dust he left behind, her fists clenched. She had that charting to do, and then she knew exactly where she was going. She turned violently back toward the hospital. In the window facing the lot, she saw Frank Meachum, smiling, waving at her from behind the glass.

"Wellesley Coe!"

The words were out of her mouth before she had the car door closed. She had spun by Midas Muffler, pushing that little

Ford to the limits of its abilities, only to have Jackie Pomeroy tell her that the outlaw she was looking for had taken the afternoon off. So now she was seeking him out in his own lair. She stomped across the potholed parking lot of the Hawaiian Sunset Apartments, a single-story, cinder-block T painted a violent orange. Wellesley's brother, Tully, was hosing off a couple of raggedy-looking potted palms, put out during the summer to lend a vaguely tropical air to the place. They were so forlorn, however, that the effect tended more toward making it look like one of those Third World sites featured on network specials about hunger.

"Tulane Coe!" Lila Mae shrieked, "Tulane Coe! Where is that brother of yours?" She planted herself in front of him, drawn up as tall and stern as she could manage.

"Why, Lila Mae," Tully said, "what brings you around?"

She glared witheringly at him and pointed at her car. Much of the dried shaving cream had blown off in her breakneck drive across town, but the legend Wellesley had inscribed was still visible in a cloudy scum. Tully turned the hose onto the cement, where the stream backspattered all over Lila Mae's tennies, as he gazed at her Ford. He smiled stupidly when he saw it.

"Hell, Lila Mae, I'd think you'd be kinda flattered," he said.

She sighed disgustedly. Tully, she always thought, was so different from Wellesley and the other brothers that she had sometimes wondered if he were a Coe at all. Potbellied, lazy, and, to her mind, dim-witted, she had never understood how he had made such a minor success of himself in real estate.

"I am *not* flattered," she barked, "I am *not* pleased. Where is Wellesley? Because I am going to tell him to his face that if he doesn't stop harassing me, I'm going to get the sheriff after him, and that's a fact!"

Tully shifted the hose slightly. Lila Mae's right tennie was now completely soaked. "Well, honey, I think if you take yourself around back, he's probably fiddling with the carburetor on Ronnie Peltz's Chevy." He directed the stream again at the dusty and disreputable-looking palms. "But I still think it oughta make you feel pretty good that a woman your age can make a man like Wellesley do such a crazy thing."

"I could not care less about your opinion, Tully Coe," Lila Mae huffed. "Thanks all the same." She stalked off toward the rear of the complex. The idea, she thought: Flattered, she was supposed to be, and "a woman your age"! What nerve! As if she were some kind of hot-tea-at-the-Old-Courthouse-Pastry-Shoppe matron! If she had been angry when she came, two minutes with Tully and that garden hose had pushed her blood pressure through the roof.

Swinging around the corner, she saw Wellesley, half of him, anyway, sticking out of the maw of Ronnie Peltz's souped-up Chevy. Why Ronnie insisted on having the car at all was the subject of considerable commentary in Rhymers Creek, in that he had the manual dexterity of a trained seal. Beyond that, he was entirely too old to be cruising down Mason Street in a jacked-up thunderer like some college kid home on summer vacation. Wellesley had his tools laid out on the fender, and seemed ready at any moment to crawl bodily into the engine. As Lila Mae half trotted toward him, she really didn't think about what she was going to do when she got there, but the logic of it was more of body than brain in any case. Bent into the car, Wellesley's long legs ended in the perfect target, and though Lila Mae had never had a ballet lesson in her life and was always a klutz in kickball, her soaked right tennie landed square in the middle of Wellesley's rump with a force that momentarily brought his feet up off the ground, and Lila Mae felt a little shudder of power as his head smacked into the upraised hood.

"Shit!" he bellowed, wheeling around, his fists bunched. On seeing her, though, his body relaxed a bit, and one hand went around to rub his bumped head. "Well, Lila Mae. That's a fine how-d'ye-do."

"My eye!" Lila Mae squeaked. "Just what kind of treatment do you expect, you . . . you vandal? What do you mean soaping up my car window? Making a public spectacle out of things? You should be ashamed of yourself."

Wellesley continued to rub the back of his head. "Now, Lila Mae. Now what did you want me to do? You won't talk to me on the phone. You won't let me see you. I just want to spend some time with you, honey, and try to make up for making you unhappy."

"Well," Lila Mae harrumphed, "you can just forget all about it. And you can forget all about me too. As if I could put up with that kind of disgraceful conduct. As if I were some common tramp! I am not the kind of girl you're looking for, Wellesley Coe, and you can just head out to Tommy Lee Henderson's roadhouse to find one that'll do that kind of thing and be prepared for it, good-bye!"

Her last words all came out in a rush, and she whirled on her heel and set out quickstep back to her car. Standing there with him in front of her, as she was talking, she'd begun to feel almost stifled. She had trouble getting her breath, and she knew she simply had to break off the conversation and run. It was those eyes, those deep-green eyes settling on her, that long lanky frame, loose-jointed and easy, the way he slowly passed his hand back and forth over his hair, slicked back and sweet with tonic—a minute longer and she would have begun to calm down, she just knew it; she would have stood there and listened to what he had to say and before she had a chance to think he would have had his arm around her and she would have forgiven him for being so presumptuous. And that was not about to happen. There were certain things a Christian woman could not allow.

Tully was still spraying the palm trees as she pulled out of the parking lot. At the very least, while she was bawling out Wellesley, he could have turned the hose on her back window and washed off the shaving-cream legend his brother was responsible for. On the road, every time she glanced into the rearview mirror, she could see it.

Before she made it halfway home, her eyes were teary, though for anger or for sadness she wasn't sure.

T W O

"That's right, Momma. A swift kick. That's what I gave him. A good swift kick in the pants . . ."

Mrs. Rudolph had tricked her again. All she'd planned to do was take that other disaster back and be done with it. Lila Mae blew on her nails, thinking the color of the polish might be different if it were dry. It looked as if that wasn't likely.

"I don't really know what he thought, Momma. And I don't really care. . . . What do you mean 'a woman your age'? That's exactly what Tully Coe said to me today. You'd think I was ready for Quiet Meadows. . . ."

It's the frost in it, dear, not the coral, Mrs. Rudolph had told her, *the frost is what's wrong. But the strong color. You've got to have it. Why don't you give this one a try?*

"Really, Momma. On 'Walking with Jesus'? That's the one

out of Dallas? . . . Now you know I couldn't possibly have. It only comes on at noon. . . . Oh, really? . . . A woman all alone in the world like you? . . ."

Lila Mae should have known anything called "Jungle Coral" would be inappropriate. It looked like something out of a vampire movie, or the kind of nail polish that one of those sultry ladies of the night on the detective shows would wear. Besides, coral didn't even grow in jungles, unless she'd been seriously misinformed in biology class. Next to them, maybe, underwater, in reefs around jungly islands out in the Pacific or down in the Gulf of Mexico somewhere. But the jungle and the coral, as far as she knew, never the twain did meet.

"Gallbladder, was it? I didn't know people could die of gallbladder anymore. . . . I know, I know. Stones. You know what I meant. . . . Like that pain you had last weekend? . . . Well . . . Oh, it's eight, and neither of us wants to miss 'World of Love,' do we? . . . All right . . . Now you watch yourself in this heat. I'll talk to you tomorrow. . . . Bye-bye."

She slipped the phone back into the cradle clumsily, in case the polish was still damp. It would likely be the devil to get off the plastic if she smeared it accidentally. She reached for her dinner, precariously wedged beside the phone on the little marble-topped table—leftover chicken with a fresh batch of Rice-a-Roni and some celery sticks—and balanced the plate on her lap. It was actually five to eight and they could have chatted a little longer, but she wanted a few minutes to collect her thoughts before the program started.

Momma had not really approved of her assaulting Wellesley today. Actually, it was battery. She remembered that from an old *Parade* magazine, where someone had written in to ask the difference between the two kinds of attacks. Assaulters you could see coming; batterers sneaked up from the back. So, strictly speaking, she had battered Wellesley today, though, despite Momma's dire predictions, Lila Mae doubted he would report her and bring suit. Wellesley, over the years, had probably absorbed considerably more than a kick in the rear from a woman more than a head shorter and sixty pounds lighter than he was.

She had already told several people about it, though it irritated her a little that nobody seemed to think much of it, and anybody who did, except for Momma, seemed to think it was cute or frisky or something like that. She had done it with all the seriousness in the world, as a sign of just exactly what she thought of Wellesley Coe. But Patsy Daniels, for example, that old roadhouse sweetheart at the checkout at Walgreen's, obviously felt that what it meant was that she and Wellesley were having a spat and wasn't that just what every man you cared about needed once in a while?

It's a world of love,
And that's why we raise our voices,
To the One above,
Who will help us make our choices,
So that when we're done
We will all be one
With that One above
In a world of love
In a joyful world of love . . .

They came bouncing down the aisles of the studio, a dozen of them, mostly fresh-faced twenty-five-year-olds who looked seventeen, though a couple of the soloists, Lila Mae always noted with relief, were a bit longer in the tooth. They simply sparkled with energy, and she often wondered how they managed to be so effortlessly cheerful with a theme song they had to sing at least twice a day, year in and year out, for however long the program had been on the air.

"And now, ladies and gentlemen, your hosts in this 'World of Love,' Ted and Becky Standish."

Ted and Becky trotted in from opposite sides of the studio, the two of them as energetic as the chorus, smiles beaming with the sheer, thrilling joy of vanquishing the power of Satan via the miracle of television, as Ted often put it. They bounded up the steps onto the stage, joined hands, bussed each other on the cheek, and shouted: "Praise Jesus!" as the crowd went wild.

Lila Mae greatly preferred Ted and Becky to any other hosts on the Christian networks. Becky had a cheerful, scrubbed look, and Ted, an easy masculinity that reminded her of the good old days at South Mockdon High. Both of them must have been about her age, perhaps a little older, but she had to admire how far they had come, after years of circuit-riding, so they often told, spreading the word all over the nation, from the quietest little town to such capitals of sin as San Francisco and Forty-second Street. It must not have been easy, Lila Mae had to admit, for the two of them to face down the crowds there at Times Square, those hookers and dope pushers and homosexuals and other people so depraved there were no polite words to describe what they did. And through it all, Becky and Ted had kept their eyes on Heaven and their feet on the ground, and now theirs was the third-most-frequently-watched program on all of Christian television, Praise God.

Tonight's featured testimony was to come from three former prostitutes from Las Vegas, along with an inspirational interview with a man cured of muscular dystrophy through prayer. Also, the "World of Love" summer telethon was in the works, with many special guests and an associated camp meeting outside the Spiritual Broadcasting Company's facilities that would feature the most astonishing array of preaching and teaching ever in the history of Christian television, all brought to you live as it happened if you were not able to attend in person. More about that later in the program. But first, to begin the evening's show, LaVonne Jackson of the WOL Singers would be premiering a brand-new song by "our very own bandleader," Mickey Olsen.

Lila Mae set her plate down. LaVonne stood in the middle of the stage in a shimmering evening gown of cobalt sequins and long white gloves, and began a slow, bluesy number apparently entitled "Bride of Jesus." It struck Lila Mae as just a tad too provocative for a hymn, but then again, LaVonne was singing it, and colored girls were always allowed a bit more leeway with that sort of thing, or so it seemed to her. It was rather pretty, and LaVonne, as always, belted it out with the conviction and lung power of a real trouper. By the end of the number, the audience was on its feet, and Lila Mae felt a little rush of emotion at the outpouring of faith and affection LaVonne's singing could draw forth. It had been years and years since she had felt that kind of mass intensity, since she was eighteen or so.

She always seemed to come back to that moment, or seemed to be coming back to it more and more: to that time when her love for Eddie was fresh, when her life seemed as full of possibilities as she could possibly imagine, when she had at least two dozen people that she thought of as friends she would keep for the rest of her days. Many of them she still saw, on the street or at the market, and from time to time she realized she couldn't imagine ever having been friends with them at all. What had they had in common? What did they have to talk about? Surely, now, if she were asked whether, say, Eliot was her friend, she could say with reasonable certainty that, no, he wasn't; he was a coworker, an acquaintance. But, in an odd way, she knew more about him after less than a month at Quiet Meadows than she had really known about those boys and girls she would have sworn undying devotion to on gradu-ation night. Perhaps that had been the problem with Eddie.

The three prostitutes from Las Vegas were spinning the story of their ascent from the pits of degradation, but Lila Mae had trouble concentrating as Eddie loomed up. She had known Eddie pretty well, actually, ever since they were twelve. His family had moved from Pennsylvania so his father could take that job at the new chicken-processing plant in Mockdon, part of the migrant wave that also brought the Hawthornes, the DiGiovannis, the Goulds, and the Garcias. She had not really paid much attention to him those first couple of years—he was shrimpy and a little funny-looking and had that unspellable Polish name: Pietrowsky. Then, just as he turned sixteen, he had what Lila Mae, in her romantic moments, called his swan summer, when he went to Pennsylvania for three months and came back changed, blossomed, made man. His hair had grown out; his shoulders broadened; he had put on at least twenty-five pounds and sprouted up three or four inches. It was an astonishing metamorphosis, and the girls were quick to notice. His invitation to the Valentine's Dance the February of Lila Mae's junior year had seemed like a gift from Heaven.

He played football, though only second string, and wrestled in the winter. His grades were not outstanding, but not bad, and his family, she was relieved to learn, had fallen away from Roman Catholicism a generation before. On holidays, they attended the new Episcopal church, built on the edge of one of the played-out gravel pits the county was trying to establish as some sort of ecological park, where they had also put up a fancy new restaurant called Macaffey's and a little nature museum. During Lila Mae's nun period, Momma had told her about the Catholics ("Give me a child till he is six and he will be mine forever!"), but in view of the fact the Pope never seemed to have gotten too good a grip on either Eddie's mother or father, much less Eddie himself, Lila Mae successfully parried a couple of such warnings early on in their relationship. Over time, Momma seemed to warm to Eddie, and Daddy as well, as much as he did to anyone who showed that kind of interest in his little girl. They had dated for more than three years, and despite the way the whole world was headed, even in Rhymers Creek, Lila Mae went to her marriage bed *intactus*. It had not been easy, there was no doubt about that, and, though it scandalized her, Lila Mae now wondered if it might not have been a whole lot better, and she might have avoided a major mistake, if she had surrendered to Eddie's ardor early on, before the date was set and the vows were said and the honeymoon was over and she had that scary feeling it wasn't going to work. At the time, it could have been explained as a youthful indiscretion, giving in to peer pressure, whatever, though she was not sure, toward the end, after she had pulled him (only temporarily, it turned out) into the clutches of the Third Baptist Church, that Eddie would have agreed anyway.

Regardless, and though she knew for a fact he had had some experience before they arrived in the honeymoon suite in

Lemon Grove, thanks to a football camp and a forty-dollar call girl over in Littlefield, they married and set up housekeeping and it all was not so bad. Looking back, it was almost as if she had spent that time in a kind of suspended animation, like something out of one of those old "Outer Limits" or "Twilight Zones." All around, the world—even Mockdon County—had been changing at a breakneck pace, but, at least for her, she might as well have been from Momma's generation, there in her little house, cooking and washing and trying to take care of her man. In the living rooms and bedrooms of Rhymers Creek, people smoked and snorted and freebased and mainlined; they swung and swapped and threesomed and grouped, and yet it all remained somehow outside her ken, something other people did, that she heard whisperings of in the same way, in junior high, you would hear about stolen kisses or somebody addicted to aspirin.

She suspected, in his times away, which grew more and more frequent, the nights out with the boys and fishing trips in the summer, that Eddie indulged in some of these activities, that more than Jim Beam passed his lips around the campfires up at the Willowood Reservoir. She had even entertained the notion of his having an affair. But she was of a formation out of synch with the times, and her growing involvement first with Third Baptist and later with "World of Love," along with, in those days, "PTL" and "The 700 Club," inclined her in a certain way to overlook that kind of thing: crosses to bear and the difficulties of the world and the temptations of Satan and so on. Eddie grew further and further away from her, and she from him, or perhaps it was that they simply grew no closer, so that after eight years of marriage to him, Lila Mae felt she knew Eddie no better than she had known him at their fourth anniversary, or their first. She prayed each night for the baby that would, somehow, make everything all right again, make the world like it was supposed to be. There was no pregnancy, and as they both approached thirty, Eddie seemed, if anything, to grow younger, to become more and more like he was their junior year, his first year on the football team, when he had gained a reputation as a hell-raiser of the first magnitude.

When it came, that note taped to the dining-room table, she missed the emptiness she should have felt, the shock, the shattering sense of betrayal and loss. It was as if she had been waiting for it, that recognition on his part as well that it was not working, that this was not what a marriage was supposed to be. Her first emotion was relief, though she never confided that to anyone, relief that all the pretend had finally run its course, even if the reason seemed to be the suggestion that, in those years she had been off the Pill, it might be Eddie's fault—if fault there was to place—that they had not brought a baby into this world.

Looking back, Lila Mae was glad of that, because she was bright enough to realize that a baby had enough to do without being made responsible for making his momma and daddy happy, that he—or she, in this day and age—had a hard row to hoe merely in becoming a person, and that insisting as well that that little child forge a bond that had never existed before was an awful thing to do to a helpless and preoccupied little thing who had never asked to be charged with such a weighty responsibility. After all the years of wishing, Lila Mae was finally grown up enough to know that you cannot ask a stranger, even one sprung from your own womb, to save something he had no part in making, even if it were that something that made him in the first place. Certain demands were not to be imposed. From it all, that, at least, was something she had learned.

Which brought Wellesley to mind. Was she expecting too much there—a man thirty-three who had never married, who doubtless had had his adventures in that new world of Rhymers Creek that had passed her by as she tried to be a woman of another age, as she tried to reproduce a notion of marriage and family that came over the airways on SBC but that, even in her own life, she had never really witnessed. She remembered crying herself to sleep, sure that Momma and Daddy were headed for divorce or worse, as Fred and Lonnie assured her and Little Joey that, no, this had been going on for years, the battles and the pettiness and the shouting; that the world, despite what the television showed, was not made up of people whose crises consisted of whether the roast had burned or whether too much money had been spent on the smart outfit featured at the local dress shop now referred to as a boutique. Loving people was hard work, often not very pleasant, and there were times you had to be prepared to pack it in, admit you'd made a mistake, not just for an evening but for a lifetime, and, too, times you had to be able to say that, yes, this was enough after all, even if it wasn't what you had hoped and expected.

But with Wellesley Coe, Lila Mae did expect quite a lot, though for what reasons she wasn't entirely sure. She really shouldn't have been surprised he was looking for a bit of fun that night. This was a man, after all, who'd spent three years in the service back in the swinging seventies. Besides, that's just how things were done these days, despite SBC and the new moralism she read about in Time. They were no spring chickens. She supposed, because she had always looked up to Wellesley as older, that all that would not be so important to him, that he would have had his fill in the extra years she still had not lived, and would be more attuned to romance pure and simple. Maybe too it was that the Coes were an old family in Rhymers Creek, people who had lived here before the boom in Mockdon County, before the population doubled and the shopping centers sprouted and Mockdon Parish was still called that and not just Mockdon, now bigger than Rhymers Creek itself.

The Coes, with the Muldoons, the Stephenses, the Mortons, the Peterses and Burneys—they had been here when the county was still dry, before the gravel pits had been opened up around Mockdon, when there was, for all practical purposes, one store where you bought one thing and then moved on to the next for your next purchase. It was before all the people came and the pits dominated the economy and Arthur Wilson made his fortune in chickens and ducklings he exported in planes to South America that, according to the local gossip, then came back crammed with cocaine for the markets in New York and California. It was a time nobody had ever heard of cocaine, when the local scandal consisted of Carrie Morton Monroe burning up her husband in the trailer left behind by her carnie lover, whom Dewey, that husband, had drowned a couple of nights before. None of that was ever proved, but it was almost as if that had been a sign that all the sins of the century were to be visited upon Mockdon County, that it could no longer be an isolated place, that lust and jealousy and covetousness had as much of a seat here as they had anyplace else in a blasted world. But back before that, back in those peaceful years of childhood, there before the Fall, even then she had known Wellesley Coe.

Of course, knowing him then was different from knowing him now, back in that time when three years made a difference, when he was a "big kid" that her brother Lonnie might play with but she could only admire from afar. Even at South Mockdon High, where he played on the basketball team, he had been too far ahead of her for there to be any real possibility of dating. Anyway, by then, the seventies were starting, and he was off to the service, and by the time he was back, she was already all but wed to Eddie Pietrowsky. During her marriage, she was proud to say, she had not looked in a serious way at any other man besides her husband, even in those waning years when she watched it go slowly to pieces before her very eyes. She had taken those vows seriously, and only when it became clear she was once again alone had she let her fantasies wander free. Still, it had surprised her a little when Wellesley Coe asked her out, as if they were still those children of a moment who felt, vaguely, they had missed something, that the history that those five or ten years older had held in their hands was somehow now passing them by. It had been a strange time to be young. . . .

But any lack of expectation hadn't caused her a moment's hesitation in saying yes.

On the tube, the Liberty Baptist Choir was thundering "What a Friend We Have in Jesus." "World of Love" was long over and Lila Mae had missed, in her reveries, the appalling details of a hooker's life on the Vegas strip. She sighed. It was probably just as well. Another sinner, another soul won for Jesus. She wished sometimes Ted and Becky would talk to somebody more like her, somebody who tried her best, who got along, whose career in this world was marred by only small failings that, nonetheless, made her feel as if she was not making the best use of what she had been given. As the first topic to be covered in the Reverend Falwell's sermon popped onto the screen in bold white letters, she turned the set off and wondered if she should call Momma to wish her good night, but thought better of it, and went, with a kind of heaviness she did not quite comprehend, to brush her teeth.

In the lounge, Priscilla stretched luxuriously and yawned. "I'm just ex-hausted!"

Billy Jean smiled. "Isn't that what the boys are always supposed to say after a long night?"

"Is that so?" Priscilla winked. "Well, I certainly can understand, you know?"

Lila Mae flipped through an old *Better Homes and Gardens* she had rescued from Mrs. McNulty's trash the previous day. Patience, she thought, give me patience.

"Well now, I hear I'm supposed to say, 'So, how far did you get?' "

"Is this when they get into all that baseball talk?" Priscilla giggled. "I never could figure that out. All that stuff about bases."

"I don't think even they've got a system everybody uses. And at your age, honey"—Billie Jean smiled—"the only thing that counts is a home run."

"That must be where score comes from," Priscilla said. "Even though you'd figure then that a triple and a single would count the same as going all the way."

"Just goes to show how smart men are."

Both of them laughed.

At your age. Your age. Lila Mae glanced at Priscilla. How old could she be? Twenty-three? Twenty-five? Why, all of a sudden, did mortality seem to be rearing up at every turn? And was it true that all men were interested in was a home run? Wellesley Coe up there at bat; and she, the ball that refused to be pitched. She made a face. What kind of ugly imagination came up with these things anyway?

"Getting to first base with me's an accomplishment," Priscilla bragged. "I'm still young enough to pick and choose."

Billie Jean wet her finger and touched Priscilla's arm. "Fffffttt! Oh, she's a hot one. But do you really have to give out free samples to make up your mind?"

"Ohhhh, Billie Jean!" Priscilla snarled in mock dismay. "One of these days . . ."

"No way, honey. That's the bargain. The pretty young thing fades away, but the bitch gets better."

Lila Mae wanted to leave. She stuck her face deeper into the magazine. What kind of a deal was that? Losing your looks and turning into Joan Collins? Besides, Joan Collins got her looks too! But Lila Mae knew that wasn't the general rule.

It was still early to start her run. Besides, on the way in, she had seen Stewart pat Eliot on the bottom in the way that even she, naive as she was, thought looked entirely inappropriate. She knew men were always doing that to each other in things like football games, for reasons she wasn't clear on and which struck her as vaguely suspect. It looked even odder in the workaday world. Besides, there was the way Stewart's hand seemed to linger there, and the way Eliot seemed to like it, that had given her the willies. It reminded her of the lawyer, Sammy Stephens, who'd handled the divorce, except that Sammy only did it with women. He was the pattiest, pokiest, touchiest, strokiest man she had ever put up with.

". . . just the hunkiest thing you can imagine," Priscilla was saying. "From Hartford, Connecticut, if you can imagine that, in insurance, and he went to Yale! I always thought those East Coast boys were all wimps, but I've got to change my tune now."

A planter made out of an old office-building ashtray—Lila Mae was deeply into "100 Ideas for Under $100"—but where on earth would you find an old ashtray like that? A lamp from your broken electric fan. A wall unit from the junked chassis of a Volkswagen. She remembered attempting some of these when she was a teenager: floor-pillow covers created out of your old kitchen rags. She had planned a set of three, but only finished one. Stuffed with some foam rubber and plastic packing material Daddy scrounged up for her somewhere, it sat in her bedroom for about two years, looking, frankly, less like "a colorful and decorative addition to any room" than one of those bag people asleep on the streets of New York she had seen on the nightly news.

"Just as long as he gave you his phone number, he wasn't married, and you had a good time." Billie Jean exhaled a drag of her cigarette and coughed lustily. "And you followed Eliot's advice?"

"What advice?"

Billie Jean sighed. "Don't go out without your rubbers."

"Oh, that . . ." Priscilla shrugged. "Well, I guess . . . He was from back east, after all. No telling, even if he wasn't a wimp."

"Don't let Eliot hear you say that."

They giggled again.

Bookends from coffee cans! (They could talk about it all so easily.) "Just fill them up with crushed stone that you can buy at your local garden shop." (Their bodies, their periods, sex, even . . . Safes.) "Brightly painted, they make the perfect addition to a contemporary ambience." (While, for her, it was

all she could do to keep from blushing just overhearing them.)
"Uncovered, you can use them for that extra ashtray at
a cocktail party." It was as if she were being tested just
working here.

"Lila Mae!"

She popped to attention.

"Do you want one or not?" Priscilla leaned out of her chair
to offer the jar of macadamia nuts, though she was still facing
Billie Jean. "I thought it was a pretty romantic little memento
from a one-night stand, especially with what these things cost."

Crunching down, Lila Mae had to admit they were good. She
had never tried them precisely because they were so expensive. The Yale man from Hartford had good taste, certainly,
though wouldn't you figure some agent of the Devil would?
Already, in her mind, he had taken on the aspect of a true cad,
come down to Rhymers Creek on some phony business which
probably had to do with Wilson's chickens-and-drugs racket,
and he would go back to Connecticut and tell them all up
there about the blonde bubblehead he spent the night with
out in redneck country.

"So, if I never see him again," Priscilla was saying, "that's the
breaks. I'm sure not running off to Hartford. And I don't see
him setting up shop in Rhymers Creek. But for a great dinner,
good sex, and a jar of macadamia nuts, it was a pretty fair
evening, all in all."

Lila Mae raised her eyes to Heaven. "Thank you, Jesus," she
whispered.

She had tomorrow off.

That week, Lila Mae's Saturday and Sunday fell on Wednesday
and Thursday. For those two days, she puttered around the

house and spent some time with Momma and went to see
Lonnie and Betsy and their new baby, Cindy, trying to be
upbeat about Quiet Meadows and her life in general though
she wasn't feeling so hot about either one. Just seeing Cindy
was, for Lila Mae, both a joy and a burden, holding the tiny
thing in her arms, feeling that grasp soft as a breath as the baby
squeezed her finger, looking at Aunt Lila Mae, and the whole
world as well, with dumbstruck wonder. Betsy always com-
mented on what a cheerful child she was, so different from the
first two, Diana and Billy, who during most of Lila Mae's visit
were involved in a screaming argument out by the swing set.
Lonnie, as usual, set her on edge with this week's parade of
purchases. It was never clear to Lila Mae how, even on Lonnie's considerable salary from the bank, he and Betsy managed
to afford such an array of gadgets. It was even less clear why
they needed half of them. In the entire year and a half they had
had a juicer, Lila Mae had never been offered fresh-squeezed
anything, and as Lonnie proudly displayed his new drill bits,
shiny sharp in a gray metal case, it seemed to her he had
shown her a virtually identical set in a blue plastic case not six
months before. Now in their third house in as many years,
Lonnie and Betsy seemed determined, single-handedly, to perk
up Mockdon County's less than robust economy, and Lonnie
sometimes made her feel almost as if she, with her limited
means, really wasn't doing her part to turn things around, for
which she should be properly ashamed of herself.

Momma, meanwhile, was suffering from inflamed corns and
some ill-defined vapors for most of the time, though she was
insufficiently distracted by her discomfort not to offer some
advice on what Lila Mae ought to be doing with herself. On
SBC, there was a lonely-hearts program—"Matching for the

Lord"—that Momma kept threatening to send Lila Mae's name and vital statistics to. After all, it would mean a free trip to the SBC studios in Charleston, South Carolina, and a chance to appear on television, where, unquestionably, an upright Christian gentleman would see her and write in and maybe they could even be part of the collective ceremony "Matching for the Lord" held every June and January to celebrate their successful pairings of good and devout people in this world of sin.

Lila Mae was not too enthusiastic about the idea, despite the fact that she was newly peeved at Wellesley for a bouquet of roses that had arrived with no card the day after she kicked him in the bottom, along with half a dozen phone calls she had had to hang up on. She was so torn by his attentions she sometimes considered merely letting bygones be bygones and giving him a second chance. It was only "World of Love" every night that renewed her commitment not to forgive what had been a gross demonstration of unworthiness and, at the very least, to make Wellesley wait good and long before she would even offer him the time of day.

Wednesday evening, she finally got a chance to read the card she had received in the Tuesday mail from Little Joey out in Oregon. That was about the best he did, a few lines scrawled on the back of the photo of some municipal building in Portland or Eugene, though at least he wrote to her on a fairly frequent basis; more than Momma or the others could claim. It had surprised them all more than a little when he up and left, though, later on, Lila Mae would think that it made more than a little sense. He had always been the least happy of them in Rhymers Creek, complaining from the moment he hit thirteen about how small and narrow and dull it was. Lila Mae frankly didn't know if she was particularly happy here, but it was the place she knew. Joey could certainly take no comfort from his oldest brother's course in life: "Dateless Fred," as Lonnie called him, with his job at Pep Boys and gambling and bleary nights of beer. Still, Lila Mae could understand how Lonnie's exactly opposite tack—marriage and family and a mortgage and a solid and secure job with Greater Mockdon County Bank and Trust— had not exactly seduced Joey either. Almost as soon as he graduated, he had taken to the open road, and she had seen him no more than twice in the last five years.

As the only one of them she could baby, she missed him sometimes, thinking back on what it was like to have Joey confide in her, to look to her for support against their parents or their older brothers. He counted particularly on her magic touch with Daddy to keep him out of harm's way and, ideally, put either Lonnie or Fred there instead. But that was all over and done, and, from what he said on those rare visits home, no one and nothing would ever bring him back to Rhymers Creek.

The slowness of her weekend did give her the chance to reaffirm in her mind just how good a program "World of Love" was. Wednesday night, she spent hours in front of the tube watching other offerings on SBC. One of the interview programs had a long report on the demonic plot that some- how involved thirty-third degree Masons and the UN, though Lila Mae found it hard to believe that a bunch of Shriners, who raised money for children's burn wards and, as far as she knew, spent their other free time riding around on silly little scooters wearing funny hats in any parade that would take them, could be part of any Satanic conspiracy. Likewise, she found equally unconvincing a special on credit cards as the Mark of the Beast, how we would all, someday soon, have those funny lines of varying widths that cereal boxes featured plastered across our foreheads. There was a Christian pianist who, in his rhinestone-studded toreador jacket, bore a disquieting resemblance to Liberace, and multiple services from vast auditoriums in Dallas, Denver, Tampa, Seattle, and Orange County, California.

The lowest blow, however, came at eleven-thirty with "Heroes for Christ," on which elaborately muscled young men prayed mightily and then broke cement blocks with their heads or lifted eight-hundred-pound weights in front of a screaming crowd of pubescent boys and girls. One boy twisted an iron bar around his neck; three together, shimmering with sweat, snapped the binding chains of sin, represented by police handcuffs, as that adolescent multitude went wild. Perhaps the oddest moment came when a cube-shaped, Mexican-looking boy spent what seemed like several minutes blowing up a hotwater bottle. The sight of that pink rubber bag bloating ever larger and tighter gave Lila Mae a peculiar, queasy shudder down near her stomach somewhere. All the straining flesh, together with the heartfelt entreaties to the Lord (Who probably had better things to do than help junior muscle men show off), struck Lila Mae as more than vulgar, as somehow almost blasphemous. When the latex bag finally exploded, the audience went into a frenzy, and Lila Mae popped suddenly out of her chair and hit the channel button, just in time to catch the late weather, which promised no relief from the heat and drought that had characterized the entire summer up to now.

Late Thursday afternoon, she finally went to see Fred.

She waited till close to sunset, when the heat was at least bearable, telling herself that, with all that blacktop, the trailer park where Fred had his mobile home would be insufferable in the full light of day. She realized that was an excuse. It was not that she did not want to see him exactly. He was always pleased when she came by, and it had been a couple weeks now since he had dropped over on Zunis to make sure she was getting along all right. He had been good to her these last months. He was always sure to make her laugh and took on some of the burden, at least, of listening to Momma's complaints. Too, of course, there was the money he'd loaned her after the divorce.

But still it was hard, she thought as she turned through the wrought-iron gateway gradually dissolving with rust, because it always depressed her to see him. The life of her biggest brother jangled inside her like a whole army of alarm bells, an object lesson in loneliness and never knowing how to cure it. She remembered him as the most rough-and-tumble of the boys, though, of all of them, she remembered him least, a full nine years older than she was. In her mind, he had always been large, almost as big as Daddy, and she had felt, even as a little girl, that that had been their problem, why they had always fought and Daddy always seemed to be after him and Fred was always in trouble for one thing or another.

At one time, she thought what had finally done him in was the war. To prove himself to Daddy, he had volunteered right after high school, and spent a full year in Vietnam. She had watched several of the specials on post-traumatic-stress syndrome, and had wondered perhaps if that was what had turned her brawling bruiser of a big brother into a quiet and withdrawn alcoholic. But it was not the awful memories of battle that haunted him, she finally realized. He had seen some terrible things, certainly, but had spent most of his time in a supply depot at Da Nang. Rather than the direct and searing experi-

ence of battle, it had been the endless stream of men and
materiel out of the base, and the endless stream of anonymous body bags back in the opposite direction, that seemed to
have chastened Fred: silenced him, shrunk him, turned him
inside himself, with no friend but a bottle. These days, Lila Mae
felt a peculiar kinship with him that made her even more
reticent about visiting. It was as if war had betrayed him.
Daddy's shining memories of the fight against Hitler, the glory
of the John Wayne movies at the Saturday matinee: those
were the images Fred bore off with him from Rhymers Creek.
And he had found them all to be meanly, horribly untrue. She
thought sometimes that his disillusion with war must be, for a
young man, very like her own disillusion with marriage. The
theater that was to make each of them a star had instead left
them with a passel of ambiguous memories, and alone.

"Well, hello there, little sister."

She climbed out of the car and into his hug. He had the
awning slung out over the concrete slab in front of his little
trailer, which threw a nice patch of shade.

"So, where have you been keeping yourself, Fred? It's been a
while since I've seen you at lunchtime."

He smiled. "I've been through a few times, but I guess not
on your days off. And now we're in inventory again."

Fred had worked for the last dozen years at Pep Boys, back
in the stockroom, where his experience in the army paid off,
and where, if he came to work a little tipsy from time to time,
it didn't make the customers nervous.

"Come on in."

"Oh, let's just sit out here," she said quickly. "I expect it'll be
cooler, and we might even get a little breeze."

"Fine with me."

She was grateful as she settled into the lawn chair. The cramped little trailer was always beastly hot in the summer, and, in the midst of this drought, would be even worse. Besides, summer, winter, spring, or fall, it always reeked of beer: fresh beer, stale beer, spilled beer, beer soaked into cushions of the easy chair, beer settled in the cracks of the linoleum, beer passed in every way a body could manage, which made her slightly ill to think about.

"Can I get you anything?" he said as he stood there in the doorway, a fresh brew in one hand.

"Just some soda, if you've got some. Or a glass of ice water is fine."

"So, how are things going at the old folks' home?" His muffled voice grated from inside. "Must be kind of a chore"—he stepped onto the drive, a Flintstones glass for her in hand— "watching out for those who can't watch out for themselves."

"Not quite what I expected it would be . . ." She gave him the abbreviated version of her weeks at work: patients and problems and the rest of the staff, a couple of funny anecdotes, Stewart and Eliot. "I mean, I just figured at a Baptist place like that they wouldn't hire any of those people."

Fred smiled. "The fruits always show up where you least expect them. That's how it was in the service. You'd figure on the swishy little clerk in the quartermaster's office, and then, lo and behold, that son-of-a-bitch lifer attached to HQ turned out to love to take it up. . . ." He cleared his throat. "Well, you get the picture, Lila Mae."

He was always deferential to her, even when he was drunk, almost protective. He was like that around all women, as nearly as she could see, shy, oddly fatherly.

"So, what have you been up to?"

"Nothing new." He shrugged. "Same old business at Pep Boys. Watching the tube. Won a hundred dollars off Binny Morton last week over at Lewie Demmers' house."

That was the one thing Fred was good at: poker. It was his one social activity, and, Lila Mae had heard, about the only place he could keep his drinking under control. He hung with a crowd aged twenty to sixty, who got together week to week, and, so the story went, he nursed a single beer for hours as his opponents at the table slowly slid underneath it. That was the reason Fred never lacked for money.

Lila Mae sighed. "You know I don't approve, Fred. But since it was that kind of money I suspect kept my head above water before I went to work, I guess I really can't complain."

He grinned at her. "Well, little sister, I'll give you credit. You're at least willing to give the Devil his due."

She greeted the comment with a little scowl, but she really couldn't be mad at him. She never could. With Joey and, particularly, Lonnie, she had never had any problem showing her temper, but with Fred, especially after he came back— even the night she went with Eddie to bail him out of jail for public drunkenness—she could never quite muster any anger toward him.

"You go over to Momma's?"

"Oh, yes." She sighed. "She wants to put me on television."

"What?"

"On that lonely-hearts show on SBC. She thinks I'll find a man if I'll only sign up for 'Matching for the Lord.'"

Fred chuckled. "You let Momma jerk you around too much, Lila Mae. Half the time I think she comes up with these things just to get your goat."

"I don't know. I guess she's pretty good at it." Lila Mae

poked him with her elbow. "Of course, I'm not the only one she leans on."

That was, she sometimes thought, their strongest bond, at least these days. Momma was always after Fred, complaining, criticizing, demanding, something he accepted with contrite patience, as if he deserved it.

"Yeah, but it's worse because you're the girl," he said. "She was always willing to cut us boys a little more slack, and she didn't meddle as much. And she never seemed to think she could figure us out the way she thinks she can you."

"I guess"—she really wasn't sure she knew what he meant—"maybe that's it."

He took a long suck on his beer can. "Ahhhhh!" he breathed contentedly. "But what about that, Lila Mae?"

"What about what?"

"A man. Isn't it about time you were in the market?"

She rolled her eyes. Why on earth couldn't people mind their own business?

"I've had some dates. But nothing serious. I need a little time. *And* the right man."

"Well, I shouldn't say so. . . ."

"You're right there."

"Now, now, don't get huffy with me, little sister." He laughed. "But it's time you were looking seriously again. Time waits for no man, or woman either."

She sighed. A fine one he was to talk. He had lived for a couple of years in his late twenties with Mary Muldoon, about as big a tramp as ever came down the pike. But after they split up, he had avoided romance altogether, and seemed to have no inclination to change his ways in the foreseeable future.

"We'll see how things work out. There just hasn't been any-body very special come my way yet."

"Nobody?"

She set her face. "Not a soul."

Wellesley Coe was there in her head, of course. Rose-bearing, forehead-kissing Wellesley, his bottom stuck up in the air out of Ronnie Peltz's Chevy. Beelzebub in a tee shirt and jeans.

It was twilight by then, though the breeze Lila Mae had hopefully predicted never had come up. In the half-light, the trailer park looked more desolate than usual, and it made her sad to think of her brother out here by himself, with his beer and poker winnings. Nobody to share things with but his little sister, who came by sometimes, not altogether willingly, and his card pals, who drank too much, and Momma, who never gave him a moment's peace whenever they were together.

"I should probably get on home," she said. "I need to rinse that uniform of mine. Back to the salt mines tomorrow."

"Well, you take good care of all those old folks." He rose with her and walked by her side to the car. "You've gotta remember that's probably where we'll all end up someday."

The notion gave her a little shiver, more for Fred than for herself, because it seemed likely he was headed toward Quiet Meadows a lot faster than she was. She just prayed that, when his time came, death might take him massively, quickly in his sleep, rather than toying with him for weeks or months or years. Of course, then there was the state of his soul to worry about.

"You take good care, little sister." He hugged her again.

"You too, Fred. Come by and see me soon."

She started the car and pulled away, looking back at his gray figure receding in the dusk. It would be a while before she got back here again. For some reason, today, it had been even worse than usual: that bleak and lonely life he lived that she was witness to and could not change.

She shook her head and turned onto the highway. She glanced at her watch. If she hurried, she might still catch "World of Love."

Back at Quiet Meadows on Friday at six-thirty, she tripped in the parking lot and skinned her knee on one of the tire bumpers, which did not auger well for the upcoming week's work. She clocked in and headed for the lounge, when, in the dim light, she thought she saw Stewart in a dress at the far end of the corridor. Stunned, and wondering whether this flagrancy was the result of some new immoral court decision she had somehow missed the report of on Christian television, she half trotted down the hall to confirm what she fervently hoped had been a mirage. Passing by Number 19, she was brought up short by Stewart's "What's the rush, Lila Mae? You got a long day ahead of you." He stood there in his orderly pants and smock, striking as a dancer, as always, his kinky hair severely cropped. Who was it, then, she had seen in that dress at the end of the hall?

She arrived at 9 and poked her head inside. There, tucking a fresh draw-sheet around Mrs. McNulty, was Norma. Lila Mae let out a little gasp.

"Norma, honey, what have you done to your hair?"

Norma wheeled around and glared intensely at Lila Mae. There was no question that it was her. Missing, however, were the mousy brown locks she was always fooling with when she was nervous, which was most of the time. They were all gone, replaced by a sort of crew cut strictly greased into a flat plane

above her forehead, the kind of haircut Lila Mae remembered
her brothers having up till they were about twelve.

"Everything's under control, Lila Mae."

Lila Mae stared stupidly. It was Norma; there was no doubt
about it—it was her figure, her uniform, that's what the name
tag said. But the voice addressing her sounded like Linda Blair
in *The Exorcist*, a deep, mannish growl, and an involuntary shudder trembled through Lila Mae as she wondered if Norma
might be possessed.

"What is it, honey? Have you got a cold?" It seemed best to
act as if this were all perfectly normal. There was no need to
put the demon on his guard just yet, until she had time to
consult with the other members of the staff to see if it was
going to be necessary to cast out some spirits in addition to all
of today's other duties.

"I'm fine," Norma growled. "Just taking care of McNulty for
Stewart."

"Okay." Lila Mae backed away.

Of course, it made sense that Satan would seek out the
weakest link in the chain, and that he'd do his choosing not
from among the staff of County General, where, as she understood it, everybody was stealing morphine, but from a respectable Baptist place like Quiet Meadows. She quickstepped back
to the lounge.

"Billie Jean! Have you seen Norma? I don't know what's
gotten into her, but it's awful." Lila Mae stood by the table
where Billie Jean and Priscilla were sharing a final cigarette. She
had almost said, "Who's gotten into her," but thought better
of it.

Priscilla, as usual, tossed her head. "Oh, cool it, Lila Mae,"
she said bitchily. "Norma's just gone over to the other side."

Lila Mae shuddered anew. It was true. Norma had fallen into the occult. It was just like Ted was always warning on "World of Love"; even worse, because with those atheist affirmative-action laws, Quiet Meadows would be required to keep a Devil-worshiper on the staff or they'd be sued.

"Oh, Lord," she whispered.

Eliot slammed into the room, his face set in a ferocious scowl and even louder than usual, muttering under his breath, "Of all the goddamn stupid . . ."

Billie Jean settled back in her chair. "Just calm down, Eliot."

"Christ!" he exploded. "Like it was like joining the goddamn Symphonette Guild or something. What a crock!"

Lila Mae was a little surprised at Eliot's concern, even if she couldn't quite approve of his expression of it. Maybe even people like that drew the line at Satanism.

"Why don't you talk to her, Eliot? Maybe you can explain it to her," Billie Jean said soothingly. "I don't even think she knows what she's talking about."

"Damn straight," Eliot barked. "If you know what I mean," he added.

"What is going on!" Lila Mae could stand the suspense no longer. Eliot seemed about the last person appropriate to exorcise poor Norma, unless he was going to pull the demon out of her by sheer brute force.

"Norma's decided she's a lesbian," Billie Jean said.

Lila Mae slumped into the nearest chair.

"Decided she's a lesbian," Eliot parroted mincingly, "decided she's gay. Just decided. Just woke up one fine day and chooses her goddamn orientation like a new pair of shoes! Jesus shit!!"

"Eliot!" Lila Mae breathed, scandalized.

"It's that goddamn boyfriend of hers," he continued. "That last one. Ricky? He told her he was breaking up because she wasn't big enough down there to take him all. That he had to find a woman who was deeper and looser. Can you imagine? I should find that stupid prick and show him just how loose and deep *he* can be."

Lila Mae was feeling a little faint. She wasn't accustomed to this kind of talk, and everything was making less, rather than more, sense as the details came out. It had seemed considerably easier when it was merely demonic possession.

"Wait!" she said, rubbing her temples. "Now let me get this straight. Norma's boyfriend told her she ... she wasn't ... woman enough for him, so now she's decided that she shouldn't be interested in boys anymore because she can't ... can't accommodate them. . . ."

"So now she thinks she's interested in girls." Priscilla yawned. "You're a little slow on the uptake, Lila, but you do clue into things eventually."

"Dumb cunt," Eliot muttered.

"Eliot, please!" Lila Mae snapped, still a little short of breath and not anxious for any more aural assaults. "But, what has she done to her hair, and why's she talking like that?"

"Because all she does is watch that stupid, fucking box, and the only lesbian she's ever laid eyes on is some cartoon of a diesel dyke on some dumb detective show." Eliot's voice was growing louder every minute. "So now she thinks if she cuts her hair like a GI and talks like a lawn mower she's found herself. It's sick!"

Norma suddenly stomped into the room. Lila Mae sighed and covered her eyes. Nervous little Norma suddenly walked like Tully Coe, though there was something not quite convincing about it, as if she were trying out for the wrong role at the community playhouse. On top of that, in the lights of the lounge, Lila Mae noted that the poor dear really did have a set of satellite dishes for ears.

Norma surveyed them all imperiously. "What's the goddamn problem?" she croaked.

Eliot let out a low moan, a sort of Frankenstein grunt, and then sidled past her. A lucky thing, Lila Mae thought; otherwise she was afraid he might have flattened poor Norma. He still might flatten her boyfriend.

The silence was overwhelming as the three women took in Norma's new look.

"Why, honey," Lila Mae said for lack of anything better, "that new haircut sure is . . . short."

"I like it that way." Norma took a step toward Lila Mae. "You got a problem with it?"

"No, no, honey. Why, the way this summer's shaping up, it should be so comfortable," Lila Mae said quickly, a smile plastered on her face. "Why, I just might get one like it myself here in the next couple of weeks."

Priscilla theatrically stifled a giggle.

"June bug up your twat?" Norma barked menacingly, leaning toward Priscilla.

Priscilla stiffened, blanching. "No. No, Norma."

Norma surveyed her with the kind of leer Lila Mae remembered from an old Johnny Carson show. "Let me know. I'll take care of it for you."

She lumbered out, raising her feet so high it seemed like she was walking on the moon. They all waited until they heard her stomp around the corner.

"What're we going to do?" Lila Mae said with an edge of desperation.

"Nothing," Billie Jean said.

"Nothing!"

"Oh, Lila Mae, you haven't been around here long enough to know," Priscilla said unhelpfully, with a smug superiority.

"What?"

"Last time, it was a nun."

"November," Billie Jean clarified.

"A nun?"

"She'd just busted up with another boyfriend . . ."

"Lennie Jencks."

". . . so she was going to run off and join Mother Teresa in India. She'd seen her on some special on TV . . ."

"Thanksgiving week. On NBC."

". . . and got it into her head that she'd been called. She nearly drove Father What's-his-name up at St. Anne's crazy."

"Father James."

"How long was it? Two months?"

"Seven weeks," Billie Jean said, playing with her cigarette butt in the ashtray. "January the thirteenth, I think."

"Then one day she'd given up the nun business, because she'd taken up with some new guy. . . ."

"Jimmy Peters."

"And that didn't last the month."

"Ten days."

"But it was enough to get her off the nun kick." Priscilla giggled.

Lila Mae shook her head. It was all a bit too much for the first twenty minutes of a workday.

"Don't let it worry you, honey," Billie Jean said, in the same soft, tired voice she seemed to say everything in. "Before her hair grows out, Norma'll be back to liking boys again. She's a sweet little thing, but Mrs. Voxburg's got more brains left in her head than Norma ever had in the first place."

"Of course," Priscilla said, "maybe this time she's finally got it right."

"Watch your twat then." Billie Jean smiled.

Priscilla blushed. "Shame on you."

Billie Jean glanced at her watch. "It's party time, girls." She and Priscilla headed for the door. "You coming, Lila Mae?"

"In a second."

She sat for a moment, utterly still. Her head was pounding. What kind of funny farm was this? Those Christmas times when she'd gotten on at Mason Hills, none of this type of thing had ever happened. It was reaching the point where Eliot and Stewart seemed almost normal. With Norma shifting from nun to Norma to lesbian, Lila Mae really didn't know what to think. She had never had to put up with anything like this before, and, frankly, she wasn't sure that it wasn't merely her soul it put in danger, but her sanity as well.

The morning was a relatively quiet one. Lee was still out with his groin pull, which meant Flaccid Farms had been divided between Lila Mae and Eliot for the duration. Norma had apparently made it a point to announce her new identity to any patient she came in contact with, so that when Lila Mae was making the beds in 34, Ellie Breckenridge keep popping up out of her usual postbreakfast stupor to say, "Norma is a lesbin. Norma is a lesbin."

"Lesbian!" Lila Mae finally exploded. "Lez-be-in, Mrs. Breckenridge!"

Elmer Wallerby, who shouldn't even have been there till visiting hours started at eleven, gave her a strange look as he passed by in the hall.

She moved on to Mrs. Voxburg's room. It was across from the kitchen, and, as usual that time of the morning, the clatter and clank of dishes, trays, and silver was almost deafening. Lila Mae uncovered the applesauce and oatmeal beside the bed and took a fresh mouth syringe out of the drawer. Alice Fitzer, who shared the room, was up, dressed, and posied in her wheelchair, maintaining an animated conversation with herself as she picked at the afghan over her knees.

Despite occasional whining, Alice was usually good company during Mrs. Voxburg's feedings. She was only slightly deaf, and had a tendency to run on at the mouth, but she enjoyed chatting and seemed to have total recall of her girlhood, which Lila Mae found comforting in somebody who had to be over ninety. This morning, however, preoccupied with Norma's transformation, she really did not feel like a social visit. Alice seemed to sense her tension, rocking gently back and forth in her chair in the doorway, watching the activity as breakfast went out and the dirtied trays came back in.

"Here we go, Mrs. Voxburg, open up." Lila Mae sucked some applesauce up into the tube and laid the tip against the old woman's lips. Mrs. Voxburg had her usual expression of terrified astonishment, but began to swallow as Lila Mae depressed the plunger and slowly fed the thick liquid into her.

As always, it made her sad. Lila Mae wondered how much of the conversation between her and Alice Mrs. Voxburg could hear, how much she could understand. Did she lie there, hopeless, her mind full of her stories, her opinions, her recollections, impossible to share with them? Did she hate them for still having the power of speech, the ability to laugh and cluck in agreement about one thing or another, some remembered adventure from Alice Fitzer's childhood or some tidbit of news Lila Mae provided? She gave no sign, or, rather, those she could give were primitive as a newborn's: a moan or a cry, a bunched fist weakly stabbing the air in resistance. She had come full circle: out of helplessness unto helplessness again. And once more Lila Mae shuddered at the unfairness of it.

As she started on the oatmeal, Lila Mae heard the kitchen door slam. They were taking their nine-thirty break, just like clockwork. She had yet to really meet Consuela, though a couple of patients had mentioned to her that the food seemed to have improved. Momentarily, the corridor was still, and Alice rolled halfway over the threshold and peered up and down the deserted hallway. Then she wheeled back into the room.

"Quiet as cotton out there," she said.

Lila Mae paused. It struck her as one of the prettiest things she had ever heard. And looking down at Mrs. Voxburg, it seemed she too was pleased, as across those astonished eyes there passed what looked like the faintest glimmer of peace.

By eleven, the bedmaking was well underway, and Lila Mae tooled into 23, her arms brimming with linen to change Mr. Ricks's and Frank Meachum's beds. Ever since she had ignored him the day Wellesley soaped her windows, Frank had been pouty around Lila Mae, though as time went on he was gradually softening. She rated a perfunctory wave this morning, better than in the past, when he ignored her entirely, though she still had not achieved the cheery-whistle status she had enjoyed before the incident. Mr. Ricks was reading the newspaper as she came in.

"Why, Lila Mae, how are you this morning?"

"Not bad, Mr. Ricks. Not bad, I guess." She stripped the sheets swiftly off Frank's bed and dumped them on the floor. "Much happen around here the days I was gone?"

"No, no, things were pretty quiet till this morning. Everybody seems to be upset about little Norma, I guess."

Lila Mae sighed. What had Norma done, published an announcement in the *Quiet Meadows Weekly Newsletter*? Or maybe she had gone all out and told reporters at the *News and Gazetteer*. "It was just so sudden, I guess. She'd had a little heartbreak and sometimes people make decisions they don't think too much about. She'll come around."

Mr. Ricks chuckled. "Well, she's been pretty dramatic about it. I just hope she's happy. One of my nephews is—what is it these days?—gay. My sister had a real hard time with it, but, like I told her, the boy seems to think it's the best way for him. Everybody's got his own direction, I guess."

Lila Mae shook her head. "I don't know Mr. Ricks. They say it's a sin, unnatural, I guess it says in the Bible. I just can't quite be comfortable with it."

Mr. Ricks shrugged. "Well, there's lots of things they say are sinful in the Bible that nobody seems to pay much mind to these days: eating scallops, getting divorced. I think it all depends on who you decide you don't like."

Stung, Lila Mae was about to say something. Mr. Ricks was taking a position diametrically opposed in a variety of ways to the one Ted and Becky promulgated, especially when they discussed their mission to the wayward homosexuals in Sodom by the Bay. And he was making comparisons that didn't seem at all fair. But after all of this morning's goings-on, she hadn't the energy right now to deal with everyday doubt and unbelief, so she let it pass, moving on to Mr. Ricks's bed, concentrating on her hospital corners.

"Much new in the paper?" she asked.

"The usual." Mr. Ricks smiled. "War, famine, pestilence, and death."

She knew it was a goad, but she was not to be moved. It was

an invitation for her to launch into a discussion of the Last
Days, something she had been particularly interested in during
the exegesis classes that had come on at ten-thirty on SBC a
couple of months back. She was certain Mr. Ricks had said
what he said on purpose, and would then argue that the Four
Horsemen always seemed to have been with us, which was a
line of argument predicted by Donnie Lawrence on the program; though, she had to admit, she had not found his count-
ers to it overwhelmingly convincing.

"Well now, you take good care of Frank here, okay?" she
said as she headed for the door.

"Okay, Lila Mae. You enjoy your day now." —he looked up
from the paper, and his tone of voice pulled her up short—
"Oh. From all the signs, you must have quite a determined
beau there, it looks to me."

She snorted. Surely Frank had pointed Wellesley's handi-
work out to him. Probably every patient this side of comatose
had heard about it, as well as the swing shift and the night
crew. "Determined but unworthy, Mr. Ricks," she said stiffly,
"determined but unworthy."

"Hmmmm." He shook his head pensively and went back to
his paper. "Too bad. It's not too often these days you see a
man so anxious to get his lady's attention."

Lila Mae bustled out. The snoopy old thing anyway. And
Wellesley—Wellesley she could shoot for holding her up to
this kind of public ridicule. As if she were the villain in the
piece, as if she were the one who was improper. He probably
knew she would never tell anyone why she had dropped him
like a lead weight. The conniving son of a bitch, she huffed to
herself. That was not the kind of language she liked to use,
even in her private thoughts, but there was no better way to

put it, no offense meant to Wellesley's mother. He should be ashamed of himself for everything he'd done, up to and including those anonymous roses. Maybe he'd realized he was betraying himself with his misspellings on the cards.

The rest of the day passed quickly enough, though the mere sight of Norma was enough to put Lila Mae on pins and needles. Half Norma's patients seemed terrified at her sudden transformation as she lumbered exaggeratedly through the halls. A couple of relatives had complained to Mrs. Lindley, but she seemed at a bit of a loss as to what to do, never having confronted such a situation before. Priscilla remarked on afternoon break that she had overheard some discussion of termination, but there was concern expressed about Eliot and Stewart: that they might quit, that they would have to be fired too to maintain any consistency, that it might get into the papers and that was the last thing Quiet Meadows needed, its financial footing never having been the strongest. The matter, of course, could be taken up with the trustees, but there again, it then might all get public and the Good Lord knew what a mess that would make.

Lila Mae was sufficiently ahead of herself that she took an extra break before her charting. Her feet hurt, which was not unusual after a day on the runs, but she wondered if they were worse because of the heat. She propped them up on the coffee table in front of the vinyl sofa. If, quite honestly, they kept Quiet Meadows a little too cool for her taste, she still almost relished her day's work to get out of the infernal weather. It wasn't merely the sun beating down day after day from a cloudless sky. It was dry enough now that the dust was up, and sometimes she would touch her cheeks or forehead and it was as if she'd put on one of those cleansers with grit Mrs. Rudolph sometimes recommended that make you feel like some ninety-five-pound weakling getting your face rubbed in the sand.

"Rough day, honey?" It was Billie Jean, her voice a lazy sigh.

"Not bad really," Lila Mae said. "But I think my ankles are swelling."

"Don't I know it." Billie Jean flopped down and put her feet up as well. "I almost look forward to the winter this time of year, except that then, my bones ache. There's no justice, in this world anyway."

The remark brought Mr. Ricks to mind, with all his barely disguised secular humanism. Billie Jean had taken out a Salem.

"What is it with Mr. Ricks, Billie Jean?"

"What do you mean?"

"Well, he's got that broken hip, but he really seems to be in pretty good shape compared to most of the rest of them in here. And the man's no Baptist, that's for sure."

Billie Jean smiled. "You know, Lila Mae, they don't ask after your religion around here if your money's green. He's kind of a sweet old guy, I think, from the little I've talked to him. Too bad he won't be with us much longer."

"Well, I suppose that hip'll heal up pretty fast for him."

Billie Jean glanced at her, surprised. "You haven't learned to read the charts when you make your entries, have you?"

"Well, no. I don't usually."

Billie Jean blew out a long plume of smoke. "Honey, that hip'll never heal right. He's got cancer. A year, if he's lucky, probably not even that."

"Oh." There really was no right thing to say. She found it hard to believe that Mr. Ricks, of all of them, was dying, that his days had a number on them, as opposed to Alice Fitzer or

Mrs. Wallerby, even Mrs. Voxburg, who might go tomorrow but might last for a decade.

Nurse Palmer stuck her head through the door. "Lila Mae, Miss Johnson is kicking up a fuss over something. Can you get her page."

Despite the fact that Miss Johnson was forever in a stew, Lila Mae was almost grateful for the interruption.

"No rest for the weary," she said, popping up off the sofa.

"No doubt about that." Billie Jean took another drag from her Salem. "Never been any doubt about that since God created woman."

Lila Mae punched out at three on the button. The first day back at work was always the hardest. After she was into the routine again, she could go shopping or pick up the groceries or even go see Momma for an hour or two. But, whenever Monday fell for her, all she wanted to do was get home, kick off her shoes, get a little something to eat, watch "World of Love," and crawl into bed. Maybe tonight she'd even treat herself to a long soak in the bathtub.

She pulled off Mason Street onto Zunis, listening to the funny noise the car had been making the last week or so, afraid it might be something costly. Even to find out if it were costly or not would be costly. She sighed. Wages at Quiet Meadows were nothing to write home about, but the economy in Mockdon County was flat right now, and, with her limited skills, not too many other prospects looked particularly appealing.

If she had seen him before she turned into the driveway, she might have simply driven straight by and gone on to Momma's house, or to the sheriff. As it was, she was so preoccupied with that noise, which seemed to change pitch when she slowed down, that her fingers were on the door handle before she noticed. For an instant, she didn't know what to do: restart the car and pull out; lock all the doors and lean on the horn, as they were always advising single women in danger to do; make a run for it on foot; stand by the car, shake her fist, and scream: "Devil, get thee hence!" at the top of her lungs for as long as it took. But finally, she just stepped out, arranged her uniform, picked up her purse (which, she noted with some relief, was inordinately heavy on account of the three rolls of adhesive tape she had lifted from Quiet Meadows today), and, with determined stride, headed for her front porch.

Wellesley Coe sat there on her stoop, all lanky six and more feet of him, a smile half-bemused, half-anxious on his face. He had been resting his elbow on one of the steps, but as she approached, he sat straight and fixed those green, green eyes upon her. Despite herself, she felt a little shudder. They really were like no eyes she'd ever seen. But weren't the Devil's eyes green? And that long, loose-limbed body, she thought, just like a snake's. Still, in his tee shirt and jeans, she had to admit Wellesley made one attractive reptile.

"Wellesley Coe," she said with feigned surprise, "whatever brings you around here?"

He cocked his head—endearing, boyish—and his grin grew more impish. "Why, I bet you just can't imagine, Lila Mae."

She stopped in the middle of the walk, about five yards from him. "Quite honestly, I can't. I've been having a funny noise in my car I was just noticing again, but I'm sure it's not the muffler. And if it's not something to do with Midas, I can't think of anything else we have to discuss."

He arched back a little, parodying her formality. "Well, there is the little question of that bruise on my butt."

Lila Mae set her teeth. "I can't fathom what you're talking about," she said primly.

"Here, I'll show you." He was on his feet in a flash, had his fly open and his jeans partway down.

"Wellesley Coe! Don't you dare or I'll never speak to you as long as I live!" Lila Mae shrieked.

He stopped with the crack of his rump just peeking over his waistband.

"Okay, honey," he said soothingly. "I was just afraid you needed your memory refreshed."

She glared at him furiously. "You know perfectly well why I did what I did. I had to use half a bottle of Windex to get that shaving cream off my back window, and a sponge of vinegar besides. Just who do you think you are to make me a public spectacle?"

He leaned back against the porch, and on his face there was the slightest hint of contrition. "Lila Mae, I wouldn't embarrass you on purpose for anything in the world," he said, "but it's been weeks now and you won't talk to me on the phone and you have Edna tell me you're busy at work and you don't even let me know if you got the flowers I've been sending. Louise Willis down at Rosies & Posies just loves to see me walk through that door these days, and you don't even appreciate it." His tone had slid down plaintively. "So, I figured finally there was no way to show how sorry I was and how much I cared about you except to make a show of it. Now I'm sorry you took it wrong, and I'm sorry it was so hard to get the window cleaned up, but I'm not sorry I did it." He smiled winningly at her. "I guess even a kick in the butt's better than no attention at all."

That smile, the way one front tooth sort of lapped over, just a tad, the other up top . . . It was all Lila Mae could do to keep her composure, to remind herself how angry she was at this man. She stomped her foot. "Wellesley Coe! You get off my porch and out of my yard this instant or I'm going straight to Mrs. Hager's across the street and call the sheriff and have you thrown off. Is that clear?"

He stood up, looped his thumbs in his belt hooks, and slumped a bit, pensive. "All right. I'll get along." he said, "But it just doesn't seem fair to me, Lila Mae. All I did was ask you if you wanted to do something men and women have been doing since the beginning of time, and I respect you for saying that you didn't. But I'll be damned if it's fair to just freeze me out for one teeny-weeny mistake like that. That's all I'm saying."

"Humph!" She bridled. "A teeny-weeny mistake! All I have to say to you is that the road to Hell is paved with teeny-weeny mistakes, and that, no, up till the Fall men and women weren't doing that, and if it hadn't been for the Fall, they wouldn't be doing it now. The only place that kind of thing's appropriate is between man and wife, and I don't think I need to point out to you that we are not man and wife, and"—her voice was rising steadily to a little shriek—"I don't think I need to point out either that the chances of us ever being man and wife is about the same as you being elected Queen of the May!"

She pointed stiff-armed toward the sidewalk, and Wellesley, after a moment's hesitation and with a thundering sigh, began to shuffle away to the street. As he passed her, he gave Lila Mae the most mournful look she had ever seen, like he had just heard that every last Coe in the whole wide world had gone down in a flaming 747, and to steel herself, Lila Mae had to pull up the image of Ted and Becky, their faces masks of horror and concern at those endless stories of lust and depravity Abner Halliday had had a fistful of: those Hollywood orgies and Nashville swapping parties and drug-ridden nights on the town in New York.

When he reached the asphalt, Wellesley turned around and said, "You just think about it, Lila Mae, that it says too, 'Judge not that ye be not judged,' and maybe you're being awfully hard on a man who was just trying to get close to you and make you happy. Just remember that."

She smirked, nodding knowingly. Always the sinner's favorite quotation. They had pointed that out on SBC. Well, she wasn't going to fall for it. She watched him lope sulkily away, awash for a moment with a certain smugness. But as his figure grew smaller and smaller in the distance, so did her satisfaction, draining away drop by drop, so that finally, when he was out of sight, she stood there beside her porch, handbag in hand, feeling that sad little emptiness she was coming to think she might have to put up with for the rest of her days.

THREE

At least this time, she thought, it hadn't been nail polish.

"Uh-huh. An Ew Patho chiwd mowester?"

This time it was lipstick.

"No. No, Momma. No, I was not making light. I don't think child-molesting is funny . . . I do not. . . ."

She set down her compact mirror. She'd been trying to see if it was even, if she'd gotten any on her teeth, if the gloss was really as subtle as Mrs. Rudolph said. So she had had her mouth kinked around a little funny and the words hadn't come out just right. Was that a capital offense?

"Momma, for Heaven's sake. My tongue just got a twisted . . . No, you never told me. . . . When you were nine? . . . But Billy Simmons was one of your playmates, wasn't he? The neighbor boy? . . . I don't know, Momma. . . . I know children can molest children. . . . Well, what did he do? . . . It sounds to me more like he just wanted to play doctor. . . . If he just showed it to you and didn't do anything else, I really don't think that counts, especially if he was only ten."

The gloss didn't look subtle at all to her in this light, and the whole shade was too red. It made her look a little frowsy. As a matter of fact, it made her look like the Whore of Babylon. She fished in her purse, sitting on the floor beside her, for a Kleenex.

"No . . . No, it's been a week. Since I found him here on the porch that afternoon . . . I suppose so. . . . If you're so curious, Momma, why don't you just go down to Midas and ask him if he's fine? . . . Since when did you get so interested in my private life? . . . Well, I'd appreciate it if you wouldn't. . . . I've got to go now. . . . I know it won't be on for twenty-five minutes, but I've got some things to get done around here before then. . . . All right. Bye."

The nerve! she thought, the nerve of that woman. Asking after Wellesley, as if she'd been enjoying all this turmoil, Lila Mae's stories of phone calls and flowers and shaving cream. Momma'd sounded downright disappointed this evening that there'd been no new developments. If she only knew, Lila Mae thought, the precise details of that advance of Wellesley's, maybe she wouldn't be so impressed with him. In her explanation, Lila Mae had been relatively vague, not wishing to bring up those devices Ted and Becky never mentioned but were always alluding to in relation to the secular-humanist sex-ed courses school districts were trying to impose on innocent kids instead of stressing the virtues of abstention and marriage. Well, Momma could just stew, as far as she was concerned. For Lila Mae's part, she was seriously considering a call to the prayer line later in the evening.

She blotted her lips once, twice, three times; inspected herself in the mirror. It wasn't much better. She studied her face in that tiny glass, so small she could see herself only in parts.

She had never been pretty. She had long ago accepted that as a given: no classic beauty, no exotic, no *Glamour* girl, not even handsome, that disturbing word they used for women who were attractive in a disturbing way, ones Norma perhaps would be dating in the not too distant future. "Pert" was the word her father used to describe her, whatever that was supposed to mean, and most other people seemed to get by with "cute." She had been cute once. But cute was a state that did not age well, and she supposed she should be grateful she had not ended up with her baby fat turned to fat, period, like a number of the other cute girls she used to know. Now, if she could be objective, what was attractive about her was a certain—what?—alertness to her features, a strength in the bones that, at best, meant that with time she would maintain her looks, indeed become lovelier, achieve a kind of mature beauty that was more precious for its rarity than the easy prettiness of seventeen. Perhaps that's what Wellesley saw in her.

She snapped the compact shut. There he was again! He was always popping into her mind at the most inconvenient times, particularly when she was thinking about herself. When she was thinking about growing old. When she was thinking about being alone. There was no disgrace in being single. She had tried marriage and it hadn't worked. But what was she even thinking about marriage and Wellesley in the same instant for? He was out of her life, over and done with, and there were other men around who would appreciate her good points—all those things Wellesley had seen about her growing more beautiful day to day—and they would be as caring and special, *more* caring and special, and they would bring her presents and send flowers and kiss her along the hairline. . . .

She sniffled a little. Damn him! Why did he have to ruin it all? Put her in a position where there was no honorable way she could stay with him. It wasn't fair.

She popped the mirror out again. She traced the line that was forming, ever so faintly, around her chin, and then, shifting the compact slightly, could see a parallel trio across her forehead. There might even have been, there near her left ear, a gray hair. . . .

It would be all right. Single or married. Every soul was special and she intended to make sure that hers was saved, no matter what her status. She had made a good and godly decision and she intended to stick with it.

Being virtuous was not all that easy in the modern world, even without the Wellesley Coes around to tempt you into sin. It had all gotten too complex and confusing lately. She somehow felt sure that she remembered a time, back in those lost days when she was small, when everyone knew his place and what was expected of him, when it was clear what was all right to do and what wasn't. In that world, there would have been no Eliots or Stewarts, no conversions as sudden as Paul's on the road to Tarsus by a silly little thing like Norma. An old man like Mr. Ricks wouldn't be in a Baptist home spouting secularist skepticism, and Billie Jean and Priscilla would be cautious to maintain a little more decorum in their conversations in the lounge. Surely, then, it would never have occurred to Wellesley to come on to her like that, and, even if it had, he would have been the one plainly in the wrong.

Then again, had she really known that world at all? She had no idea what grown-ups were really doing back then. Maybe it

wasn't that Carrie Morton Monroe had had an affair that was
the big deal, but that it was somehow public, and things got
out of hand, and both her men ended up dead. All Lila Mae
had to go on was her memories of Momma and her friends, of
what they were shocked and not shocked about, though even
then, how honest would they be before their daughters? All
she knew was how she was told to act, what was proper for
her to do, which she got from Momma and the Baptist Church,
home ec and the biannual girls' hygiene class. But that those
sources really reflected a reality, rather than ideals, she wasn't
entirely sure.

She switched on the television. Instead of the singers bouncing down the aisles, Ted was sitting alone on a spotlit stool,
sort of like, she remembered vaguely, Perry Como used to do
on his program. He was speaking very earnestly, and she leaned
forward to turn the volume up.

"... that this ministry, in the times we are living,
would inevitably be the object of scurrilous rumors. Our time
has come. Becky and I knew, even in those days before we
appeared on the airways, that the Devil would try to beat us
down, and, sure enough, right in the moment of greatest success, when we are saving souls for the Lord daily—not one or
two, not a dozen, but fifty, a hundred, five hundred—he has
made his move. I believe we're being tested, and we should
have known that the Great Deceiver himself would wait till we
had reached the pinnacle before he arose to try and cast us
into rubble.

"Now I know that, in the past, we have come to you, our
friends across this great nation, for support for our broadcasts,
for our missionary work, for our tent meetings and crusades
from California to the New York Island. I know you have given

freely to do the Lord's work, our work, even if it meant a little
extra sacrifice at home: skipping that trip to the beauty parlor
or watching that game on television instead of buying those
expensive seats. But I must tell you now that, because of these
rumors, which are completely baseless and false, our pledges
have fallen to an all-time low, and if this trend isn't reversed
very, very soon . . ."

Ted's chin began to quiver—that square, manly chin that had
made him one of the most photogenic of the televangelists—
and his eyes misted. The slight catch in his voice that had been
growing more and more noticeable now struck him dumb altogether. He lowered his face to his hand for a moment to
regain his composure.

Of course, Lila Mae had seen him cry before. Ted and Becky
were not as weepy as some of the other stars of SBC, but from
time to time, after a particularly moving testimony or an unexpected miracle, they would let loose with some honest Christian tears. It was healthy, Ted had explained once, for us to be
open about our emotions, especially when we were involved
in the Lord's work, given He could read our hearts anyway.
Lila Mae felt herself get a little choked up, though she was
confused. Somehow she had missed this crisis that now threatened to destroy the Standishes' ministry.

Ted raised his head again, but did not speak. His eyes were
closed, and there was an unexpected tranquillity in his expression. Suddenly, he trembled violently.

"Kawasanda meleyhee neenuki soya. Palameya bokoko
malandi opopo exeselta mowanda regi, losotso papoya wannani.
Exzeem soya. Lositsi . . ."

The Spirit had entered him. Again, this was rare for Ted and
Becky, unlike some of the Pentecostals she occasionally caught

who seemed to be able to summon up the Holy Ghost like clockwork after twenty minutes of preaching. But Ted and Becky only occasionally spoke in tongues, which to Lila Mae always sounded like some unknown African language or Hawaiian, like that old joke she saw on tee shirts sometimes: "Komoniwannalayya." Ted had once spoken in baby tongues: a kind of "goo-goo, gaa-gaa" thing, and Becky had exploded on one program in something that bore a suspicious resemblance to pig latin. Still, despite her Baptist roots, which inclined her to take a dim view of charismatic excess, Lila Mae had never quite found it in herself to reject the notion of tongues out of hand. God, after all, could presumably decipher just about anything human beings could come up with; so, as long as you were sincere, it probably didn't make too much difference what language you said something in.

"Ahhhhhh!" Ted let out a long moan and shuddered again. The Spirit had apparently departed. He now smiled out at the audience, spent but somehow relieved as well.

"Oh, could you feel it? Could you feel how the Holy Ghost came down? This really is a blessed, blessed mission we have. A special one in the eyes of God. But, to continue it, we need your support. Please, right now, go to the phone. We have operators standing by to accept your pledge. Whatever you can give, more than you can give! Have faith that the Lord will provide for your needs and help you provide for ours. Fifty dollars. Fifty dollars if that's all you can afford. A hundred. Five hundred. We need your contribution now if we're to continue this ministry. Without you, 'World of Love' cannot survive. We can preach and preach, but without your dollars to pay for the satellite time, without those nickels and dimes which allow us to bring our message into your home day after day, the screen will go dark, and then Satan will have won another victory in this battle of the Final Days. If you don't have the money on hand, remember that we accept VISA and MasterCard. Just give us your credit-card number and we can put those funds to work right now. Call. Our pledge number is right there on the screen. If you have trouble getting through, praise God that there are others like you committed to saving this ministry and try again and again till you *do* get through. Our address is there as well, but please, if you can, call in your pledge. We need your assistance right now if we're to survive as a ministry and continue to battle the forces of darkness which are loose in this world right this very moment as I'm speaking."

In the background, there was a wild jangling of telephones, and Lila Mae had a sinking feeling one of them might have Momma at the other end. Six months ago, Momma had sent Ted and Becky three hundred dollars for their foreign missions project, a tour that took them all over Europe and the Middle East. Since it was not too long after she had sent one hundred dollars to Jerry Falwell and fifty each to Paul and Jan, Jim and Tammy, and the Reverend Schnook in Amarillo, Lila Mae and her brothers had threatened to talk to the bank about counter-signing her checks. They really hadn't been serious, and Momma had accused them all of being greedy and just waiting for her to die so they could divvy up her estate, which, Lonnie had unkindly pointed out, would hardly set them all up in the lap of luxury. Still, she had stopped talking about taking a new mortgage out on the house to have some cash on hand. Lila Mae had suspected those bills would be in her purse only briefly before winging their way through the miracle of VISA cards to SBC studios in Charleston.

It wasn't that she thought Ted and Becky didn't need the

money. Surely all that television time was expensive, and you couldn't expect the business of saving souls to come cheap. But it bothered her a little that they were always bringing the subject up. Money was another of those things, like sex, you really weren't supposed to discuss in polite company, and from time to time it did strike her that on "World of Love," and a number of the other programs besides, they seemed to talk of little else. Whatever the topic was, you could be pretty sure that lust and the almighty buck were going to enter into the discussion eventually.

Becky had joined Ted now, obviously deeply moved by his appeal. Her eyes were red-rimmed; though, thank Heaven, she was not addicted to mascara and eye shadow like certain other evangelical figures, so she looked truly overcome, rather than like a major disaster at Barnum & Bailey's. Indeed, she looked rather like the winner of a beauty pageant, right at that moment they're putting the crown on her head, when she's already gone through the shock of hearing her opponent's name announced as first runner-up, and is smiling through her tears of joy. Becky's presumably weren't happy tears, but they did make her look stunning.

The WOL Singers appeared, though not quite their usual sprightly selves. They were taking the theme at a somewhat slower tempo than usual, which gave it a sober and melancholy sound. It was as if they were warning that audience that, if the funds weren't forthcoming, that bounciness it was expecting would be replaced by the somber tread of a funeral. Tonight's program's feature was "The Miracle Report," an update on healings, transformations, and financial coups achieved through the power of prayer, most often in conjunction with Ted and Becky.

As the series of video clips began to roll, Lila Mae found her mind beginning to wander. There was one segment about a lesbian who had found the Lord and was now the mother of a beautiful baby boy. Lila Mae thought briefly that it was too bad Norma wasn't tuned in, but the likelihood of that seemed slim. So far, she seemed to have had no second thoughts about her sudden conversion to same-sex relations, despite Billie Jean's and Priscilla's prediction. Eliot was still furious about the whole business, though he did seem to be keeping his anger more and more to himself. Lila Mae found his attitude a little confusing, in that Ted and Becky were always emphasizing how the poor homosexuals, since they couldn't have children, were always trying to convert normal people to their perverted way of life. It was like some sort of antichurch, or so it seemed to Lila Mae, faggots out proselytizing for unnatural sex instead of the Lord. She would have thought Eliot would have been thrilled to death that Norma had become a lesbian, though, admittedly, he would not accrue any sort of benefits from it on the physical side. But, as she understood it, homosexuals of whatever stripe, male or female, stuck together, hatching plots to subvert the schools and the military and the Supreme Court. What really threw her, however, was how anybody could fall for their line, if, as Ted and Becky (together with every homosexual who had ever appeared on their program or any other she had seen on SBC) said, that kind of sex was so repulsive, repugnant, disgusting, unsatisfying, and degrading that all it could lead to was disease, despair, alcoholism, drug addiction, and suicide. Why, she wondered, would anybody let himself be talked into it in the first place, or if for some reason he did, persist in something so grossly vile and unpleasant? Another one of those mysteries of the Devil's ways, was about all she could come up with.

Ted made another plea toward the end of the hour for increased funding, asking especially that those who had already pledged earlier in the year make a second faith gift, which would earn them, for the men, a cross-and-Bible lapel pin, specially cast in copper, and for the ladies, a genuine silver-plated praying-hands lavaliere. As Becky modeled the latter, Lila Mae could already see it hanging around Momma's neck. At the program's conclusion, with the pledge phone number and the VISA and MasterCard symbols flashing at the bottom of the screen, the WOL Singers returned with an upbeat rendition of "This Old House" featuring, particularly, LaVonne Jackson, who, to Lila Mae, looked a bit strained this evening, as if the whole business of this scandal of murky details was taking a toll not merely on Ted and Becky but on the rest of the members of the WOL family as well.

The segue into the "World of Love" theme was barely over when the phone started ringing. As Lila Mae expected, it was Momma.

"No, I hadn't heard anything about it. . . . Just yesterday? . . . Well, not on the SBC news . . . Since when have you been watching Dan Rather? . . . Why didn't you say something? . . . Really? . . . I can't believe that. I just can't. . . . Not Ted . . . With a beautiful wife like that? . . . I know, I know. Of course it's been happening all over. But still . . ."

She would have to pick up the *News and Gazetteer* tomorrow. They were sure to have a story on it. Don Belmon was an old atheist—everybody knew that—and that son of his, Willie, who'd come back to help run the paper after his father's stroke, had spent five years on one of those East Coast papers, so what could you expect? They'd have a field day. Nonetheless, Lila Mae could not keep from feeling, along with regret and the

fervent hope those rumors all were baseless, a real and profound anger. If this was true, how could they? Both of them? It
simply had to be trumped up, and yet, look at Jim and Tammy.

"Well, Momma, we'll just have to see. . . . I know. It is
hard. . . . But maybe it is lies. You know, those reporters get all
excited over something and, with all that's been going on,
they're liable to make a mountain out of a molehill. . . . You
just pray; that's right. . . . Yes, Momma, I will too. . . . Okay . . .
Okay . . . I love you too. Good night, Momma."

She sat for a moment, the phone dead in her hand, long
enough for the dial tone to come on, long enough for it to turn
into that honking that tells you you've left the receiver off the
hook. She leaned forward slowly to put it back on the cradle,
almost knocking the little marble-topped table over in the
process. It was just too much. That Ted would be accused of
that kind of thing: graft, secret gambling debts, sexual adventures not only with strangers but with members of the staff,
hints of threesomes and pot-smoking. She shook her head.
How could he? And Becky too. Becky supposedly knew all
about it, had her own secret bank account and an affair with
Jerry Crylon, the singer who often guest-hosted the show when
Ted and Becky were away on a crusade.

It was all just rumors. And yet, here in the last months, all
those kinds of rumors had turned out to be true. Her throat
constricted, and suddenly her hands were clenched. This hadn't
come over her in a long time, since the early days with Eddie,
when she first realized it was all turning out wrong. Even then,
the feeling had been less rooted in Eddie than in the fact that
marriage itself seemed to have betrayed her. And that was what
she felt: betrayed. It was like finding out your uncle had mo-
lested your little girl, or that your son was taking money from

his brother. Ted and Becky had encouraged people to get close, so close, to them, to look upon them just like they would the people next door, like they would look upon kin. She and Momma talked about them with the same kind of ease they would talk about Lonnie and Betsy, more easily, in some ways, than they talked about Joey or even Fred. "World of Love" had become a kind of social call, one they expected to make every evening, one they would compare notes on afterward, just as you would with a friend who happened to have dropped in on a mutual acquaintance the same day that you had. And now, now it turned out that they hadn't known Ted and Becky at all.

Lila Mae tried not to prejudge, but she had this intuition it was going to get worse, that more would come out and it would be even more damning. And she knew, as a Christian, she should find it in her heart to forgive, and yet, it would be so hard, so very hard to do it in this case; forgive these hypocrites who had begged and cajoled the pensions and Social Security and hard-earned cash saved for a little luxury out of Momma and the old ladies like her, out of lonely people who looked forward every night to the inspiration and happiness Ted and Becky would bring them, and most of all the company, the feeling of belonging, having someone. . . .

She caught herself.

It wasn't just Momma she was thinking about. Or other old ladies. Lila Mae realized it was she herself. She was the lonely one there in front of the screen. The one who'd withdrawn from the world and built her evenings around a television program that promised to make her feel special and loved and part of something larger. Could she really feel so sorry for Fred, after all? He had his six pack and she had SBC.

A woman her age . . . That's what Tully Coe had called her, and her very own mother. Since Eddie left, she'd turned into an old maid, had been turning into one, really, for years before he finally left that note. Waiting for a baby to make her alive again. And that was no way to go through life, Lila Mae Bower Pietrowsky. No way to go through life at all.

Two days later, she finished the marketing and put a little mulch on the petunias in the flower bed. She had hoped to mow the yard, but by midday it was so hot she knew she'd have to put it off till evening if she didn't want to risk sunstroke. She'd picked up a *News and Gazetteer* at the store, and, with a glass of iced tea, sat down to read the latest gory details in black and white.

It was more or less as Momma had outlined it. There had been whisperings for years, it turned out, and one of the South Carolina papers, along with a TV station in Charleston, had been putting the puzzle together piece by piece for the last several months. Lila Mae very much wanted to believe it wasn't so, but even in the article patched together from the wire-service stories, the evidence looked pretty overwhelming. People were willing to make sworn depositions, it seemed, and there were contradictory financial reports, apparently incriminating correspondence, even some taped telephone conversations. Things did not look at all bright in this World of Love. But Ted and Becky denied everything, and insisted they would fight back, to save both their good names and their ministry. Lila Mae sighed: film at eleven, no doubt.

The doorbell rang. She thought it was probably Fred, who took his lunch about now every day and might have actually hit her on a day off this time, though, to her chagrin, the possibility also floated through her mind it might be Wellesley, come back to try to make amends again. Hard as it was, she was still determined to turn him away. He hadn't pestered her recently, but he probably thought that Ted's and Becky's problems might soften her up a bit. She would show him, she thought as she reached the doorway; he could just . . .

"Hello, Lila Mae."

She stood stone still, and she could feel the surprise across her face.

"Hello, Eddie."

"May I come in for a minute?"

She had her hand on the screen door, though she wasn't certain whether she was pushing it open or trying to hold it shut. A strange numbness coursed through her, till finally all she trusted herself to do was stumble back from the threshold.

"Of course. Come on in, Eddie."

He followed her back to the kitchen, where her half-drunk glass of iced tea sat next to the paper. He stopped by the table, while she continued all the way to the corner of the opposite side of the room before she turned.

"Ah . . . would you like some tea?"

"No. No, thanks."

"Coffee? I can heat some up."

"No. Really. I can't stay long."

"Oh. Okay."

There was a moment when neither of them spoke. Lila Mae remained rooted in the corner; Eddie by the table. She had not seen him in months, at least close up, had not really talked to him since before he left the note. She knew more or less what he was up to, of course. This was Rhymers Creek, after all, and big and busy as the county had grown, most of that newness was centered up at Mockdon. In Rhymers Creek, people still kept an eye on each other. There had been the business of the divorce, all amicably handled, all done through Sammy Stephens, since neither one was contesting. Her brothers ran into him occasionally, and Momma had several friends who knew the Pietrowskys and kept her up on Eddie's doings, more or less. Lila Mae had even spied him a couple of times herself across the parking lot at Mason Hills and once downtown. But it had been almost as if he were dead, as if the stories of his present she heard about him were the same as she could tell about his past, as if that man getting out of the Chevy truck was somebody who sure looked an awful lot like Eddie from a distance, didn't he? Now here he was before her, and she was as speechless as she would have been before a ghost.

He was still a handsome man, in an odd way for this part of the world. The blond hair and ruddy complexion were unremarkable, but the paleness of the blue of his eyes, the slightly turned-up nose, the cheekbones that, he told her once, must have come from some raping Tartar centuries back, all gave him, on close inspection, the aspect of an outsider. He stood there looking woefully uncomfortable, and, for the life of her, Lila Mae couldn't imagine why he had decided to come by.

"So, you're getting along?" he said.

She nodded. "Yes. Good enough. I'm working now."

"I heard." Eddie shifted his weight from foot to foot, like a little boy, like she remembered him doing over the years. "Your brother, Lonnie, told me over at the bank, I think. Quiet Meadows?"

"That's right."

"How is it?"

"Not bad," she offered neutrally. She was a little shaky. This was too unexpected, too peculiar. "What was it you needed, Eddie?"

"Well, I came by to tell ... I mean, I thought you should know ..." He would not look her in the eye. His gaze went from the floor to the ceiling to somewhere over her left shoulder, as if there was in the corner a cobweb she had missed. "I ... I'm getting married."

"Oh."

It came out in a small, soft voice, after a hesitation that was just seconds too long, long enough for her to know that Eddie had heard it sure as a sharp intake of breath. A funny chilliness ran all through her, and it was as if she were winded. For an instant, she could say nothing more, her mind a blank, her tongue like a brick in her mouth. The man she loved once and loved no longer was telling her he had found someone else to love and to love him, and though it would never have occurred to her in her wildest dream to ask him to come back, the realization he would be forever beyond her beckoning was, for the space of a heartbeat, almost enough to kill her.

"Well, ah"—her right hand fluttered up, birdlike, with a mind of its own, before it settled at the base of her throat—"how nice for you, Eddie."

"I wanted to tell you myself." He was talking too fast. "I only proposed yesterday and I didn't want you to hear it from somebody else, Lila Mae." The words falling out in a stumbling rush like an apology, though what, Lila thought, did he have to apologize for to the woman he was divorced from, after all? "I wanted you to hear it from me. Understand?"

She nodded. He was a good man, Eddie. He was just not the man for her, that was all. And he would never be hers now. Never, ever again. "Of course." Then she added, almost as an afterthought, "Who is it?"

"Oh. Oh, yeah. It's Mary Gonzalez. Remember her? Pete Gonzalez' little sister."

"Sure. Sure, of course." Lila Mae had not moved. She remained there in that corner of the kitchen, almost wishing the wall would open up and swallow her, let her fall through into some other dimension. Or, failing that, that Eddie would go now.

"I . . . I gotta get back to work, ya know?" It was as if he read her mind. And maybe he had, from the almost decade they had shared together, understood the signs and the gestures, or had merely imagined before he ever came what her response would be and had determined to make the announcement and then leave, as she would want him to. He began to sidle toward the door. "I'll just get along now. Don't want to be late. But I wanted to tell you myself."

"Uh-huh." She nodded vigorously, her arms clamped around her like a straitjacket or a life preserver. He was almost to the threshold, almost to the hall. With supreme effort, tensing herself almost more than she believed she could, at the instant he was slipping past the jamb, she said forcefully, a little too loud but without the slightest quiver, "Congratulations, Eddie. Congratulations."

Then he was gone.

The smack of the screen door reached her ear at the precise moment she felt the first tear slide down her cheek. Oh, God, oh, God, why now? She did not need this with all the other things that were going on: trying to live her life and forgive Ted and Becky and understand why one of her coworkers had become a lesbian overnight and deal with all the other queers and crazies at work and keep Momma from coming unglued and avoid Mrs. Rudolph's fashion advice and get the image of Wellesley Coe finally and definitively out of her head.

Mary Gonzalez. A Catholic girl. Momma had been right! One way or another, if you were born to it, the Pope got you in the end, even if he had to use a little Mexican floozy to do it. The Gonzalezes had come at the same time the Pietrowskys had, to work in that damned chicken factory Arthur Wilson had founded and made millions on and was making millions more on now bringing in drugs from Colombia. Well, it was good enough for both of them. Mary had been a little tramp even when Lila Mae and Eddie and Pete were still in high school and she was only twelve; even then she was making eyes at the senior boys like she expected to be marching beside them at graduation. And now here was Eddie robbing the cradle, taking up with some eighth grader. A spic and a pollack! It was just the kind of match you . . .

She started to sob. What was she thinking? What kind of old, bitter shrew was she becoming? What kind of Christian thought those kinds of thoughts? She reached for the dishtowel on the counter beside her and gave herself over to the sadness, wondering whether Eddie would make Mary the kind of husband he had never made himself for her. That maybe now he had grown up enough to be responsible, or maybe Mary would be less demanding, more understanding, a better wife and helpmate. And maybe they would have a baby, the baby she and Eddie never had.

Slowly, she got a hold on herself. She held the towel, cool

and damp, against her face, and dabbed at her eyes, snuffling and trying to forgive herself for striking out, even in her own head, at Mary, who was a pretty girl and worked hard, so they said, down at the window at the post office, and at Eddie, who if he was immature was still man enough to come to her to tell her what he must have known would be hurtful news, but news she should hear from no other lips but his. It took courage to do that, and decency, and a kind of caring that maybe she had never given him credit for when they were married.

She pulled in a deep breath. The house was close in the afternoon heat, and she knew now she should do something to be busy, to keep her mind preoccupied so she would not think of what had just happened. But the paper did not beckon, and the marketing was done. She could call Momma, but that might be the worst thing she could choose. Three days ago, she might have dialed the prayer line at "World of Love," to talk to one of their counselors and pray and feel the sadness lifted off her. But even Ted and Becky had failed her now, and she quite honestly did not know where to turn.

"You sure you're okay, Lila Mae?"

It was odd how accustomed she had grown, in such a short time, to Norma's new voice. As if since she first came to work there had been a crew-cut, gravel-voiced diesel dyke (an expression she had picked up from Eliot) on the staff. The dithering little peabrain who always seemed on the verge of tears had been erased sure as chalk from a blackboard, and it was occurring to Lila that, regardless of what she'd always been told, that might not be such a bad thing.

"I'm fine, Norma," she said. "Just a little tired."

They all had noticed. She had never been so glad to be back at work as that week, and yet, everything that had happened on her days off stayed with her. She knew she was quiet and listless and mopey, and about the only thing she could find to be encouraged by was how those people at the hospital, whom she really hadn't known that long, seemed to sympathize with her, even though they really had no idea what the problem was. She wasn't going to pour out her heartaches on the job. It wasn't just Norma, or Billie Jean, whom you'd expect that kind of thing from, but Eliot, who'd covered for her without a word one morning when she had fallen seriously behind, and even Priscilla, who off the rag was none too pleasant to her but, these days, seemed to make an effort not to snap.

Still, that was a minimal ray of light in what seemed daily a darker and darker existence. She was hopelessly blue, and yet really couldn't think of what to do about it. Perversely, she continued to watch "World of Love" night after night, though each broadcast seemed shriller, more desperate. Tongues came to Ted till she thought he would bloat from the Spirit, and Becky had acquired a sort of zoned intensity that reminded Lila Mae of Hamlet's girlfriend in the film of the play she'd seen in junior English. The bounciness of the WOL Singers now seemed, at least to her, peculiarly jerky, as if they were all on some kind of drug. Even LaVonne had developed, in her singing, an edge to her voice Lila Mae didn't remember hearing before, a kind of metallic hardness signaling someone gradually spinning out of control. Sometimes, deep in the La-Z-Boy, she thought it was a little like having a ringside seat to watch the sinking of the Titanic.

To make matters worse, Momma talked like she was determined to go down with the ship. She floated the idea of taking out a home-improvement loan and then sending it off to Ted and Becky; she wondered aloud how much that diamond ring and earrings she had from Daddy's mother might bring from a jeweler; she speculated on how much she could raise "just to have some money for an emergency" from a yard sale. Lila Mae had estimated seventy-five dollars tops, a figure Momma had not been pleased with. Lila Mae thought she had gone a bit high.

In the midst of such riveting goings-on on the national airways, Lila Mae's mention to her mother of Eddie's wedding plans made hardly a ripple. "Well, what did you expect? After you drove him out it makes sense he was going to find somebody else, doesn't it?" was about all the sympathy she had to offer. It was not precisely what Lila Mae needed to hear, though, of course, what *did* she expect? Eddie had a life to get on with, as did she. But at that precise moment, simply coping with it day to day seemed to stretch her energies to the limit.

To make everything worse, Wellesley was letting her alone. At least, she thought, he might have continued his pursuit of her, so she could feel desired and appreciated even if she had no intention of surrendering in the slightest bit to those emotions. She could have hoped somebody else would ask her out, of course, that as yet undiscovered clone of Wellesley Coe who was a born-again Christian. But he hadn't shown up, and she frankly hadn't the energy to look for him very hard at this point. She did find herself thinking an inordinate amount about Wellesley these days, more, in fact, than she had when he had been bombarding her with roses and phone calls. She would notice a man's hands drumming on the counter at the pharmacist's and think that, my, he had long fingers just like Wellesley. Or she would be standing in line at the market and a waft of

Vitalis would suddenly hit her from the man ahead in line and she would get almost misty. On the way home from work, she would see the bottom half of a man sticking out of the front of a car and would take a second look on the chance that it was Wellesley, giving her another opportunity to express her displeasure over . . . over what? The most public declaration of a man's love she had ever received? Why, she thought, did such a devoted and beautiful man have to be immoral?

The constant worrying inevitably showed on her face, and, at least she suspected, even in the way she held her body. She had always had good posture, but she caught herself slumping more and more. Not just the others on the staff, but the patients began to notice a change in her. Alice Fitzer's strolls down memory lane while Lila Mae was feeding Mrs. Voxburg were few and far between, and even Mrs. Voxburg seemed unnaturally cooperative, her ever-frightened eyes bulging as if she were confronting an axe murderer. Elmer and Heck had rung Lila Mae only twice during their latest visit, the first time about getting a pitcher for an iris they'd brought their mother, probably, Lila Mae thought, snitched out of somebody else's garden. She had apparently been so grumpy they had really waited too long when they paged her again to take Mrs. Wallerby to the bathroom. The poor dear was on the verge of blowing up. Lila Mae knew she was being short with everybody, and yet there seemed nothing she could do about it. She would be consciously pleasant for a few minutes, but then would forget herself, let the sadness rise up, and was mean as a wet cat again. It really wasn't fair to the patients, who had so recently had to deal with Norma's alteration from Poor Pitiful Pearl to Telly Savalas, to now have to confront helpful, Christian Lila Mae transformed into a raging harridan.

It was Mr. Ricks's bath day again, and she rattled into the room with that hideous chair, trying to muster some spunk despite how she was feeling.

"Off to the showers!" she warbled lustily, though even as the words were leaving her lips, she realized that might not be the cheeriest thing to say to an old person who remembered World War II. Her only consolation was a reasonable assurance Mr. Ricks was not Jewish.

He looked up at her benignly from the magazine he was reading. Frank Meachum was over in the closet, grubbing around. Lila Mae knew she should find out what it was he wanted. He really oughtn't be in there fiddling with things on the shelf. But it could take five minutes to figure out precisely what he was after, and she did want to get Mr. Ricks in and out and done with so she could chart and be on her way.

"Well, let's get you into that shower!" she said with false heartiness. "We'll get you all cleaned up and fresh." That was probably exactly what they told people as they were herding them into the gas chambers. "So you'll be all set for entertaining the ladies this evening." That lightened things up a bit, but what on earth was she saying? "Down in the parlor," she added, as if he was going to sneak some woman into his room like this was a college dormitory.

He extended his arms and she reached under his armpits and had begun to guide him out of his chair when there was a deafening clatter as one end of the closet shelf gave way and boxes and crates and a couple of pairs of shoes all rained down on Frank Meachum.

"Mr. Meachum!" She was across the room in three seconds. "Mr. Meachum!"

He was leaning against the wall of the closet, white as a

sheet, dazed, breathing a little hard. For an awful ten seconds or so, she was sure he had had another stroke. Still, on closer inspection, he looked none the worse for wear. She took his arm, but he shook her loose, managing a quick little whistle to show he was all right. Then he casually bent forward to sort through the desolation he had wrought.

"Oh, no you don't, Frank Meachum!" Lila Mae felt a burst of fury explode somewhere down in her middle, shooting like a rocket to her head. She grabbed him roughly by the shoulder. "Frank Meachum, you let that stuff alone! Look at the mess you've made! Just look! You get along now and leave us to our business here. Get on!" Mr. Meachum's face possessed three times the terror it had after the avalanche of boxes. Lila Mae could feel the veins in her neck and temples popping out. "Go away and let me clean up this mess. Just go on! Shame on you!"

He pulled away from her, amazed, and it took him an instant before he regained a degree of composure. His dignity was sorely wounded, it was obvious, and yet he was hardly able anymore to defend his honor, even against an assailant the size of Lila Mae. He cast her a withering glance, as close to the evil eye as she had ever seen, and then made his way slowly toward the hall. On the threshold, he turned, drawing himself as straight as he was able. Then, with a single, piercing whistle, his good arm shot up from his side, and he gave her the finger.

It took a moment for the gesture to sink in. Then Lila Mae bolted after him. He'd get a piece of her mind! She stopped herself at the jamb, however, and felt a little sob working its way up out of her throat. She slowly leaned against the door, swinging it shut, and then sat back on the foot of Mr. Meachum's bed, giving herself over to tears.

She'd been crying so much recently her eyes itched all the time. At home, the littlest thing sent her over the edge. Switching channels, she happened on an AT&T ad about some poor man who had chosen the wrong phone system and looked like he was on his way out of the company sooner rather than later, and she began to bawl like a four-year-old about his predicament. Ted's and Becky's problems set her off on a jag every night, and the sight of virtually anything she and Eddie had bought together—the toaster, the bath mat, the bedside lamps—gave her a lump in the throat. The other day on "Jeopardy," the correct question to one of the answers was "Who was King Midas," which, of course, reminded her of Midas Muffler, which reminded her of Wellesley, and she was on her way. But at least, up to now, she had managed to do her weeping in private.

"Lila Mae." Mr. Ricks spoke very softly. "Lila Mae."

There was work to do. Mr. Ricks had to have his bath. What was she doing, breaking down in front of this old man all but naked there in front of her? She shook herself smartly and reached over to Mr. Meachum's night table for a Kleenex. She blew her nose and blotted her eyes.

"Well, Mr. Ricks," she said with a thin imitation of normality, "let's see about that shower."

"Lila Mae . . ."

She put her forearms under his armpits again and gave a lunging tug. He didn't budge.

"Now, what's the problem here. Mr. Ricks, you've got to help me out." She felt the strangling sensation she suspected a psychotic killer feels just before he commits an unspeakable crime he will not remember. "Let's get those feet up and we'll be on our way."

She reached down and patted his thigh. He grabbed her hand.

She almost shrieked. What was he going to do? Force her to touch him or something?

"Lila Mae!" he said forcefully. "We are not going anywhere. Now just sit down!"

Confused, and terrified, she tumbled back against Mr. Meachum's bed.

"Listen to me," he said sternly. "The most important issue right now is not my bath. Stewart can give me a bath tonight. I'm a night owl and that boy doesn't have near enough to do when he's here. Besides, I think he likes to try to shock me with all the stories he tells, half of which I don't believe. So bathing can wait. What cannot wait is what's bothering you. You're a changed woman the last few days and I think you better try telling somebody why."

She was so stunned that, for a moment, she could think of nothing to say. So it wasn't her virtue that was at stake; it was her privacy. She sat straight and looked at him haughtily. "I don't think, Mr. Ricks, that there's anything in my job description that requires me to share the details of my personal life with my patients."

He snorted. "Oh, for God's sake, missy, who's requiring you to do anything! It just seems to me you've got the prickles worse than most anybody I've ever seen, and in my day, at least, the only way to get out of a state like that was to talk about it with somebody. Now it's pretty apparent from what I pick up from Norma and Eliot that you haven't breathed a word about what's eating you to them, and from what I can see, you haven't done it either with anybody outside this place. So, Lila Mae, here's an opportunity to get everything off your chest with an old bird who probably won't be around very long to embarrass you about anything anyway." He smiled, coaxing, trustworthy. "Come on, Lila Mae, you can humor me a little. Make an old man feel useful."

One part of her mind told her to stand up and walk out of that room without so much as good-bye and inform Eliot and Norma, those blabbering tattletales, that from now on they could be in charge of Number 23, and another part told her to throw the old geezer a bone or two to make him feel like he was helping her out. But even as she weighed these alternatives, her mouth was moving, and word after word came tumbling out about this and that and the other, all in a sequenceless jumble. Poor addled-looking LaVonne and Mrs. Rudolph and her cosmetics and Wellesley almost mooning her in her own front yard and Momma's endless problems and what to do about Norma and the whole thing with Fred was so sad and Eddie getting married again and Wellesley not calling or anything and her suspicion that a good half the time anymore Ted was faking those tongues and Wellesley making her a public spectacle with that shaving cream and why couldn't Eddie have found a girl from out of town she'd never heard of, some flashy ex-stripper or something, so she could at least feel that he had never been any good and she could never have made that marriage work and why was it Wellesley had to be so pushy that night, if only he'd held off a little more maybe her conscience would have been easier about things, and "Oh, Lord, I'm just so, so tired. . . ."

By the time she was done, he was patting her hand, and she had started to sniffle again. It was almost as if it were years and years before, and there had been some crisis. The boys wouldn't let her play, or maybe later, when one of her friends had made some catty remark about a dress she'd worn or how she wasn't going steady. She would try to talk to Momma, but Momma, somehow, did better with her brothers, pushing Lila Mae instead to accept what came, to pay whatever it was no mind, to know her place or to keep her upset to herself. Then it was Daddy she went to for comfort, Daddy who would strap the boys for complaining but never raised a hand to her, who would sit her down and hear her out and assure her everything, finally, would be all right, and that she was the best, the finest, the most perfect girl that had ever been created in the history of time.

"Well, Lila Mae," Mr. Ricks said quietly, "it sounds to me like you've got plenty of reasons to be a little on the edge these days. That about right?"

She nodded.

"Now listen, honey. I'm not real good at giving advice to people, and half the time it's a waste of breath anyway because they never listen, and I sure didn't for most of my life. I'm not going to pry into whys and wherefores about all these things, but it seems to me there isn't much you can do about a lot of them. Your Momma's your momma, and she's been the way she is for a good long time and you're not gonna change her, I suspect. And that man you were married to is going to marry somebody else pure and simple, and there's nothing you can do to change that, and I don't know that you'd want to if you could. But there are some of those other things you can do something about. You can ignore them, or you can think them out real careful, or you can just do what your heart tells you to do. But the important thing, Lila Mae, is to do something."

He smiled at her, and squeezed her fingers. It wasn't very

profound advice—she knew that—but it was somehow comforting all the same.

"I'll tell you something, Lila Mae," he said. "Over my time in the world, I guess the one thing I learned is that it's better to do what you want, what you feel, and regret it afterward than it is not to do it at all and then always regret it anyway. I don't suppose you ever heard of Richard Halliburton?"

She shook her head.

"Well, this is sort of a silly story. But, in a funny way, it makes my point, I think. Back when I was a boy, years and years ago, there was this Englishman, or maybe he was American, an adventurer, I guess he was, a kind of professional tourist almost, always going off to these exotic places and meeting people and taking some pictures and then writing about it. He published three or four books. There was one called *The Royal Road to Romance*, I remember, and another one, something about South America. But anyway, I read them all when I was a boy, and I thought to myself how fine it would be to travel all over the world and know all those mysterious and wonderful places.

"But times weren't good and I got interested in other things and pretty soon I was married and had a family to support, and sometime in the thirties Richard Halliburton died and I pretty much forgot all about him. Then, back in the fifties, I think, my youngest boy brought home a book from the school library that he'd picked out. And it was called *Richard Halliburton's 'Book of Marvels.'* It was a big oversize book with lots of pictures, but still a little too advanced for my one boy, so I told him I would read it to him night to night before he went to bed.

"And that's what I did, for a week or two, and so I got to go back again to all those wonderful places I'd read about years before and still had never seen. There was Timbuktu and

Mecca and Constantinople and Manaus. And reading about them then, that second time, I knew I'd probably never see them, and that made me very, very sad.

"The hardest one of all—you'll think this is funny, but this is true—was the story Richard Halliburton told about the Taj Mahal. Now as far as I know, he might have made it up, but what he wrote was that he went to see the Taj Mahal, which had been built by some maharajah or other for his favorite wife, who was very beautiful and who died very suddenly. And he was so grieved that he built the Taj Mahal to bury her in, even though he nearly bankrupted the whole kingdom to do it. He had planned another building just like it, but all black, on the other side of the river, where when he died he would be buried, and there would be a silver bridge between the two tombs that would link them together forever.

"But his son overthrew him and he was killed, I guess, so there was only the Taj Majal, all white marble and beautiful gold work and precious stones. And gardens. Beautiful, beautiful gardens full of flowers and shrubs and quiet pools of water. Richard Halliburton went along describing all these things, and then . . .

"Then he told about how, in the evening, as they were closing the Taj Mahal, he hid. I can't remember where he said it was, but he hid and they didn't find him, and maybe he even fell asleep. But he didn't come out of wherever it was he was hiding until it was very late. Everybody had left. The place was deserted. So he wandered all over, and finally went outside. As he was standing there, the full moon started to rise, and the whole Taj Mahal was lit up with a soft blue light and since it was so white itself it shone just like the moon did. And in the gardens, he came upon one of those pools. So he stripped off all his clothes and let himself, very gently, into the water, and swam." Mr. Ricks's voice rose at the end in a high, sweet whisper. "That's the thing, Lila Mae, that I'll always regret. That I never swam naked at the Taj Mahal."

When he finished the story, there was utter silence. Lila Mae could have cried, but she didn't, because there was something about what had happened that had moved her in a way tears didn't quite address. She did not know quite what would. After a moment more, she stood up, pulled her hand away, and then gently, sweetly, as she might a baby, she kissed Mr. Ricks on the forehead. Then she turned and walked out the door, with a sense she was bearing with her a pearl of great price.

FOUR

"Is that a fact, Momma?"

Tonight, she had no nail polish, no lipstick. Nothing new to
try to make herself look more beautiful.

"I just can't see Jerry Falwell saying that."

She'd gone to Mason Hills today like always, expecting to drop
by the Walgreen's and find Mrs. Ruldolph there at the cosmetics
counter, ready to talk her into trying yet another kind of paint
she really didn't need. But, instead of the smiling, soft-voiced,
gray-haired lady she expected, always immaculately turned out
and oh, so pleasant you just couldn't say no to that fragrance
she was particularly taken with this season, there was some little
thing not even old enough to drink, rouged up like a French
streetwalker, trying to tell ladies who'd been buying makeup
there for thirty years what they should and shouldn't use.

"He must have been angry about it, I guess. Probably figures it reflects badly on the whole bunch of them."

It really didn't make much sense. Minus the lacquer, that girl was a pretty little thing, at the age when, frankly, a little lipstick and maybe a dab of blush on special occasions was all the help she needed. With all her complaining and despite all the money she threw away on cosmetics, Lila Mae trusted Mrs. Rudolph eventually to set her right in a way she simply couldn't some slip of a girl who, at least for the moment, was natural peaches and cream. It turned out, to Lila Mae's relief, that Mrs. Rudolph was merely on vacation, off to visit children or grandchildren or both for a couple of days. Lila Mae made it clear she was just browsing to the adolescent Tammy Fae at the counter, and left not long after with nothing but a new Kleenex dispenser.

"Well, Momma, it's hard to know. No, I don't think I'm going to watch. . . . Really, I haven't watched the last couple of days. . . . It just makes me unhappy, so I don't bother. . . . I'll see if there's a movie on, or read. I picked up some best-seller at the checkout stand. . . . Let me know. . . . I'm sorry, but it's just too depressing. . . . Okay . . . No, you wouldn't want to miss it. . . . Bye-bye."

It was one of those things she'd decided she would do, as Mr. Ricks had suggested. One of those things she could change. The decision to stay away from Ted and Becky at 8:00 P.M. might not seem like much of a big deal to most people, Lila Mae thought, but for her it was significant, a complication she was removing from her life, thank you. She would not have sent them out in the cold, probably, if everything on "World of Love," or everything in her world, which could use some, had been A-OK. But as it was, she had enough problems of her own without having to try to deal with Ted's and Becky's endless and increasingly hysterical pleas for money.

The last straw came the night she got home after Mr. Ricks had told her that odd little story about the *Book of Marvels*. LaVonne Jackson had looked absolutely cadaverous during her solo, utterly strung out on—Lila Mae fervently hoped—the sea of troubles lapping the decks of "World of Love," rather than upon any of those mind- or mood-altering substances Ted was rumored to be a devotee of. Becky had turned into a kind of zombie, a doll-like creature who spent most of the program sitting down, smiling, with an occasional eruption of baby tongues. Ted himself was visited only sporadically by the Spirit, at least that particular evening, but had acquired a peculiar petulance he had never exhibited before. He was "seeing" quite a lot on the other side of that screen, primarily un-grateful people who had experienced a miracle in their lives due to the efforts of "World of Love" and yet had not become contributors to its worldwide mission, even in this time of peril.

"There's somebody out there, I can see you now, a woman, a woman who for years and years has suffered from back troubles. Oh, those pains. Those pains were just excruciating, just too much to bear. And then one night, it was last month, no, two months ago, here on 'World of Love,' on that night we had a healing right here in the studio, that woman put her hand on the screen . . . and then . . . and then . . . Kawansanda hototi magawara soya itsetsi . . . then she felt the healing power of the mighty Word coursing over the airways, through the atmosphere right here out of our studios and across this great land of ours, into her house, her television set and through it into her and she was . . . batanda fodoshee manani latta, rekitsee ammara soya . . . she was healed! She was healed! Praise God! Let me hear you all. Praise God! Praise the Lord!"

Out of the studio audience, there was a chorus of hallelujahs, of "Praise God"s and the hint of some tongues here and there. In the background, Becky was off on her own private prayer session in a language yet unknown.

"But that woman, that woman who is watching right now, after those years of pain which were ended in the split second of a miracle here so recently, has she given thanks? Has she shown the Lord the gratitude you would expect for His grace, His healing, His miracle visited upon her life . . .?"

Ted's handsome, strained visage clouded. A sinister, dark light seemed to stream from his eyes.

"No," he breathed in a strangled whisper. "No. No! No! She has not! She has not given thanks for this wonderful gift of the Lord. Maybe her faith was not strong enough. Maybe she could not bring herself to believe in the miracle that God wrought upon her. Maybe she was tested after her healing by being filled with those spirits of doubt and unbelief ever present in this world, ever watchful for that weak and defenseless human soul that has not truly accepted Jesus into his heart. Come back, sister! Come back. Even now this ministry which brought you into contact with God's healing power is under assault by the forces of darkness. Do not be fooled by the Great Deceiver. You who have seen God work in your life, help us now."

His arms were spread wide, as if to embrace that penny-pinching lady with a history of back trouble who was holding out on "World of Love."

"Now you might say: 'All right, Ted. You're right. I'll call right now and pledge fifty dollars.' " He pursed his lips and closed his eyes, shaking his head. "Nope. Nope. That won't do.

You need to pledge one thousand dollars. One thousand! Now I hear you. I hear you now: 'Ted, I just don't have that kind of money. I wish I could help, but I just can't.' "

Again, that face darkened as with a shadow. "Can't? Can't! Alone, no! No, you can't, if all your trust rests in your puny power. But if you have faith, if your faith is not in yourself, not in this world, but in the next, then yes, yes, you can pledge that one thousand dollars! What's that? Five hundred? Nope. No. One thousand! That is what the Spirit is telling me. One thousand. One thousand dollars to assure that our battle against the demons which beset this ministry and each and every one of you can go forward. One thousand or nothing! Now there's another person out there, a man . . ."

Quite honestly, it had shocked her. Ted and Becky had surely passed the electronic collection plate before, but this time, there was a meanness to it she had never seen, at least so baldly. Ted was talking like he was some sort of real-estate agent, like a broker who was demanding his commission. As far as Lila Mae was concerned, the miracle healing was something between the particular lady with that particular bad back and God, and if Ted had had anything to do with facilitating their getting together, that was fine, but it didn't seem exactly Christian that he should be whining about collecting his fee.

So, this evening, instead of "World of Love," she found an old movie with Lee Remick and Steve McQueen, for whom, she realized with a slight shudder, she had always felt a certain lust in her heart. In the film, he was an aspiring country-and-western singer ex-con—a kind of Abner Halliday who had gotten all the wrong breaks—and Lee Remick was his long-suffering wife. From the beginning, you knew it was going to end badly, which it eventually did. It was not a great movie, but easy enough to follow without paying too much attention, which was what Lila Mae needed at the moment. If she had wiped Ted and Becky off her list of problems, she now needed to decide what she could do about certain other things in her life.

The one she kept coming back to was Wellesley Coe. That error-admirer. That man with those green, green eyes just like the Devil's, tempting her to do something immoral, assuming she would, that she would be prepared. And yet . . . What was it she wanted? What did her own heart tell her to do, and didn't that count for something? She could end up, after all, years and years from now, just like Fred had remarked, stuck in a rest home, telling some girl not even born yet how she had never realized the one thing in this world she most desired. Or, worse, rather than like Mr. Ricks, she might be like Mrs. Voxburg, lying there, perhaps full of warning, of counsel, and incapable of uttering the least word of it to those strangers who kept her mute body alive. Maybe Wellesley was that pool of water at the Taj Mahal, and if she didn't plunge in, heedless of the consequences, she might regret it the rest of her life. If she didn't take that chance, she would never know.

It was too complicated. Lila Mae merely wanted to do right and be happy, which seemed a less and less easy task. She watched glumly as, sure enough, Steve McQueen botched his chances for freedom, stardom, and everything else and ended up in the slammer again as Lee Remick rode off to a life of loneliness and poverty. She glanced at *TV Guide* and sighed. On UHF, they'd been showing the Marx brothers.

That night, it happened again, as it had sporadically these last couple of weeks. She had not really fallen asleep, but, rather, was right at sleep's border; still, dreamy, and alone on top of the sheets against the heat. She could not tell, while it was happening, if her eyes were open or shut; distinguish what was occurring in her mind and what before her there in the bedroom. In the dimness, she saw a man, tall and slender. She could not see his face. He had his back to her, covered with a tee shirt, and he was whispering, but she could not make out the words. Then, the voice would grow louder, more insistent, though what it spoke was no clearer. She would feel her skin grow unnaturally dry, and she tried to reply, but nothing came out of her mouth. The man's hands would move slowly up and down his body, vanishing from her view, then reappearing in the black. She would hear the purr of a zipper, the clank of a belt.

Her own hands would caress her arms, her sides, her breasts. She would strain to see, but all she could make out was the white cotton of the tee shirt, which was suddenly rising, shrinking, and then disappearing through the air off to a hidden corner. The voice would be gone, replaced by nothing more than breathing. Her own breath would grow louder, more ragged. She suddenly would not know whose hand it was that stroked her skin. . . .

Then, shivering, she would start up out of bed, bathed in sweat, certain it was all real, and she would start to call out. But she would catch herself. Some part of her mind would not allow it, and she would then slip easily, trembling, into a mysterious sleep.

When she arrived at Quiet Meadows next morning, Stewart and Eliot were all aflutter in the corner of the lounge. That was not really accurate, she realized. Actually, they were just talking kind of low between themselves, with a gesture or chuckle now and then. But whenever she saw them together, especially after that little butt-patting incident, she immediately viewed them in the dimmest possible light, despite her own best intentions. Even if you wouldn't necessarily peg either one of them, especially Eliot, as "that way," she couldn't help but interpret their every move as broadcasting their gross, unnatural, and perverted way of life.

Billie Jean and Priscilla were at the table, smoking, as usual, grabbing that morning nicotine rush that would have to last them for a couple of hours, until the morning rituals were done. Lila Mae thanked the Lord she had never become a smoker. If being a Baptist had done nothing else, it had spared her that addiction. She had noticed how anxious both her coworkers became if they did not get their breaks at the normal time. Even Billie Jean, ever imperturbable, started to get a little funny around the eyes if she didn't get her cigarette between nine and ten. Lila Mae sat down at the far end of the table. They were talking about cars, and, again as usual, about men.

"If he has a Trans-Am," Priscilla was saying, "I just tell him I forgot my lipstick in the ladies' room and leave him flat in the parking lot. I don't know if that car does something to them, or only that kind of man buys that kind of car. But the second that motor goes on, their hands go off the wheel and up your dress. I've been through too may near head-on collisions to put my life at stake with some sex maniac who thinks his car and his dick are the same thing."

Lila Mae blushed. Billie Jean nodded.

"Since Phil and I split up," she said, "I haven't gone out that much, you know, with the kids and all. And even when I do,

I'm not much of the pickup queen I used to be. But I remember when I was out with my friends, especially Milly Worsley, Ike and Alice Worsley's girl, who was born right around the time Ike died, before Alice married Roy Holland, who's on the board at First Presbyterian now . . ."

Frequently, Billie Jean never finished a story, or, rather, the story she finished had nothing to do with the one she started, her memory taking her on such elaborate detours that she ended up counties away from where she intended.

Priscilla made a rolling gesture with her hand.

"Anyway, Milly always told me to look for a man who drove a Dodge. She said that Dodges weren't flashy, that if you were looking for a good time, pick up a guy with a Chevy; if you really were just out for a roll in the hay, pick a guy with a truck. But if you were in the market for husband material, always go for the guy with the Dodge."

Lila Mae wondered fleetingly what she was to make of Wellesley, who had an old Camaro and a van. It unfortunately looked like he was a hybrid—a good-time, roll-in-the-hay type—which was not exactly what she needed to hear right now.

Priscilla shrugged. "I don't know. And you can never tell in the bar who's driving what. Maybe the guys ought to have to wear one of those sticky labels with a decal of their hood ornament on it."

Billie Jean laughed. "There's about as much chance of that as their having a label telling you what any of their other ornaments is like."

They both giggled, and Lila Mae felt uncomfortable. Norma clumped into the room.

"Morning," she grumped. "How's tricks?"

There was a dull ripple of greetings from the table. Stewart, however, popped out of his chair. "Norma. Norma, when are your next days off?"

Norma looked at him suspiciously. "Monday. Monday and Tuesday. Why?"

"Listen"—Stewart took her by the arm and guided her over to Eliot—"we're going to drive down to the capital on Tuesday to see some friends. Why don't you come too? We can all go to the Capitol Caucus and dance."

"What's the Capitol Caucus?" Norma asked warily.

"Just about the only decent bar in this whole godforsaken state," Eliot grunted. "Come on, Norma, if you're gonna come out, you might as well do it right. There's a lot of women like you who come to the bar. You might meet somebody."

"Say you'll come," Stewart begged. "Please, Norma. It'll be so much fun, and there's somebody really special I'd like to introduce you to."

Lila Mae's temples throbbed. So it was happening after all. Eliot's initial fury at Norma's transformation was only a show. He and Stewart had just been waiting to make sure her conversion was sincere, and now they were going to introduce her into those mysteries of degradation that would ultimately end with poor Norma overdosing on pills or throwing herself off a bridge. A couple of weeks before, she would have made the effort to save the poor addlepated thing, but as it was, Lila Mae would have to leave Norma to her own devices. She did cast Stewart a murderous glare, as if to say that, though Norma might be taken in, she knew the Devil when she saw him.

Norma looked unsure, the first time Lila Mae had seen that in some time. Obviously, Stewart was calling her to put up or shut up. "Well, ah, I mean . . . I don't know. I'll have to see. Ah . . . I've gotta work the next day."

"Don't worry. We'll get you back in time. Or maybe you could trade with somebody. Hmmmmm, ladies?" Stewart looked from Priscilla to Billie Jean to Lila Mae. "How about it, girls?"

If she had just walked in at this point, Lila Mae knew she would probably have volunteered. But seeing what the plans were, she simply would not be party to Norma's ultimate perdition. She set her face in a ferocious scowl and concentrated on Eliot's motorcycle boots, which he still had not exchanged this morning for his tennies.

"Oh, I'll cover for you," Billie Jean said. "Go on and have a good time with the boys. Just as long as you pick up my shift Sunday. That'll give me a three-day weekend."

"Terrific!" Stewart smacked his fist in his palm, then took Norma by the arm and led her out toward the hall. "Norma, you're just going to love this place, it's so . . ."

Lila Mae snorted scornfully. Priscilla whipped her head in her direction. "What's your problem, Miss Priss?"

"Oh, nothing. Nothing at all," Lila Mae said huffily, standing up. "I just decided I wasn't going to be the one to encourage Norma in all this. Lord knows, she's got enough problems already without . . ." She glanced over at Eliot, who was watching her with an amused half-smile. "Without getting involved in . . . in that kind of thing."

She would have said what she meant, but, oddly, she found herself too concerned about Eliot's sensibilities to get the words out. There was no point in throwing up to him that she knew he was a miserable sinner who would lead a dreadful and unhappy life and then burn in Hell for all eternity. It was probably her Christian duty to try to save him, but he certainly didn't seem interested in being saved, and she hardly had the strength right now to drag anyone that large back to the straight and narrow.

He shrugged and began unlacing his boots; removing his tennies from the gym bag next to him. "Well, Lile, I don't know. Maybe we just ought to let Norma go in headfirst and see if she likes diving." He smirked at her. "If you know what I mean."

Both Billie Jean and Priscilla giggled, and Lila Mae was so angry she felt like smacking him. "Eliot! Eliot, you are just impossible!" she hissed, turning on her heel and marching directly out the door.

Her time on the runs did not go badly that day. Ellie Breckenridge was planning another one of her picnics, while Mrs. Wallerby seemed to be in a reflective mood.

"I . . . I . . . I don't really m . . . m . . . m . . . mind the b . . . boys coming by. R . . . re . . . really I don't," she confided as Lila Mae was making the bed.

"Well, they seem nice enough, certainly," Lila Mae lied.

"It's j . . . j . . . just that I ca . . . ca . . . can't stand them while th . . . the . . . they're here," she said flatly.

Lila Mae turned with a little hoot of surprise, looking over at that shrunken old woman whose face was creased with the expression of a little girl who has just said something very, very naughty. After an instant's hesitation, both of them broke into conspiratorial giggles.

Frank Meachum was still cool but correct with her. She liked to think he was a little embarrassed for having flipped her the bird the other day. Mr. Ricks was pleasant, and not nosy at all, for which she was grateful. At lunchtime, she'd been tempted to take Norma aside and try to talk her out of the expedition to the capital, but thought better of it. It was time she minded her own business for a while. There was considerable truth to the notion that you had to make sure your own house was in order before you put yourself to straightening up anybody else's, and there was little doubt she still had a good deal of heavy cleaning to do before she'd be ready to mop up Norma's life.

About the only difficulties that arose were with Mrs. Voxburg. She hadn't taken much of her breakfast, and as Lila Mae sat there with her strained vegetables and pureed beefsteak and crushed rhubarb at one o'clock, trying to keep one ear cocked toward Alice Fitzer and her long story about playing the spoons when she was twelve, she felt a vague disquiet settle in her stomach. Mrs. Voxburg seemed oddly droopy, her head lolling, choking on her food. Lila Mae reached over several times to massage her throat, help her get the substanceless mash of what they served her and what she could stomach down her. What kind of life? she thought. What kind of life is this for someone who must have had one once?

After she rinsed the mouth syringe and put it back in the drawer and pushed the tray away, she looked down into those cloudy, half-closed eyes and stroked her palm over Mrs. Voxburg's forehead.

"Awful tired today, honey?" she cooed. "You need to take a little rest so you can eat your dinner. You just get a little sleep now, okay?"

It seemed so futile. Could she understand anything at all? But at least she could feel that hand across her skin, at least—at best—she could hear the tone of voice, that soothing sound that, Lila Mae hoped, came over with the sincerity she felt. She sat there for a minute or two, watching those eyelids dip gradually more and more, till she was certain Mrs. Voxburg was asleep.

•   •   •

After work, Lila Mae took the long way home so she could stop downtown. After years of somnolence, during which it hardly merited the name, downtown had slowly begun to shake itself awake again. The boarded-up storefronts she remembered from her adolescence had largely disappeared, and if it seemed like the only kind of business that ever had the money to set up shop was yet another bank or savings and loan, there were a couple of new shops scattered here and there. Probably the most important innovations were the twin apartment towers on the site of the old Harley's Hardware and Appliance and the refurbishing of the Old Courthouse as an office complex with an overpriced restaurant and tearoom on the first floor. As a courthouse, it had been replaced by a sinister-looking pile of tilting concrete slabs that looked like the ruins of a building after it had been stomped by Godzilla, which sat all by itself just outside the town limits on the main route north. Of course, it could have been worse, in that there had been a serious attempt to move the county seat lock, stock, and barrel up to Mockdon. The new location was a compromise reached between the boosters there and the town fathers in Rhymers Creek, who said there would be blood in the streets before they agreed to let the upstarts at the pits steal the seat of government away.

She window-shopped at Letting Loose, the boutique Mel and Bel, the Beauford twins, had opened up. She frankly couldn't imagine how they made a go of it. Most of the clothes were expensive, and far more experimental than most women in Rhymers Creek were inclined to shell out good money for. Of course, both of them had rich husbands, and it was possible that Mr. Beauford, who, as soon as his father died, had sold the family shoe stores to one of the chains and made a bundle, then went to fat and had two heart attacks, had helped out as well. After that, she wandered over and bought an ice cream at the frozen yogurt place that had opened where the old Rexall's had been. She sat down in the dying light to slurp it on one of the benches in the park beside the Old Courthouse, where she could see the people come and go and figure out who was feeling flush and who wasn't.

"Well, well. What brings you down in these parts?"

Even before she turned to face him, she knew it was Sammy Stephens. She knew the voice, of course, having dealt with him during the divorce. But beyond that, she could have predicted he would be here. It was legendary in the county how, every evening, Sammy took a constitutional around the park and, weather permitting, enjoyed a cigar on one of the benches. He was an old-timer, who had refused to abandon his apartment and office here downtown even when it meant he had to drive for miles to go to court now. He came up to her and squeezed her shoulder.

"Mind if I sit down?"

"Suit yourself," she said, shifting over a little to give him plenty of space. Sammy was a famous lech; he had been one for years, though, oddly, the overtness of his reputation almost gave him a kind of charm, and a dispensation to do things other men might have gotten slapped for. Since he was now in his sixties, his age probably had something to do with it, but, nonetheless, it was also affected by the real egalitarianism of his lust, directed toward anything in or potentially in a skirt, which had become a sort of Mockdon County tradition. No woman worth her gender would show her face in public if, at some time, she had not received a pinch, pat, or poke from Sammy Stephens.

"So, Lila Mae. Decided to soak up some of the bright lights of our booming city center?"

She smiled. "Just having a look at what the twins were trying to foist on all of us this season."

"Naugahyde, I think." Sammy took a drag on his cigar. "They're big into Naugahyde for fall."

She didn't know quite how serious he was being. It was one of the things that was a little disorienting about him. When she was a girl and asked her father once what "irony" meant, the only illustration he could give her that made sense, now anyway, was that it was the way Sammy Stephens talked half the time.

"Cat got your tongue?"

"No. No, I was just thinking how I'd look dressed up like a restaurant booth."

"Pretty strange, I imagine. Strange stuff. Strange girls." Sammy shrugged. "Of course, they come by it honestly enough. Finelle Beauford was about the wackiest momma anybody ever had, as near as I can tell, and Seedy Beauford never knew to come in out of the rain."

"Well, he did know enough to sell his father's shoe stores."

"A lucky break. He'd have been in bankruptcy court in two years, sure as I'm sitting here."

She smiled. He really was outrageous. A curmudgeon, she thought—about the only time in her life she'd ever thought of that word. It was so hard to imagine he had ever been young.

Sammy took another puff. "I hear your ex is set to hitch up again."

Lila Mae sat straighter, a little tremble of violation passing through her. This was not a conversation she wanted to have.

"So I hear," she said coolly. "I wish him well on it."

"I expect you would, Lila Mae." It sounded sincere, "Of anybody whose divorce I ever handled, I expect you would. But what about you?"

"What about me?"

"I'd think you'd have a gentleman caller or two to call your own."

Lila Mae opted for a joshing tone. "Shame on you, Sammy Stephens. You know a woman shouldn't kiss and tell."

"Again, least of all you." He nodded. "But just you make sure you take care of business. You don't want to end up like Freddie, all by himself in that goddamn trailer with no partner and no possibilities." He stilled her objection with a shake of his head. "Now I hear you're working out at Quiet Meadows, which is perfectly decent and all, but it's not good for a girl like you to spend all her time around old folks. Why, look at you here with me!" He stood up. "You just be getting on with things now that Eddie's taken care of. That's over and done."

She felt stifled, and yet she didn't feel she could snap at him. Sammy could be a tiresome old gossip—she knew that well enough—but she knew too he didn't mean what he said to hurt her, that, never having married himself, having handled divorces for years, he took romance seriously in a way that only those people who have never really been in love can do.

"Well, I'll do the best I can, just for you," she said teasingly.

He smiled at her, then reached down and took her hand, brought it to his mouth and kissed it gallantly. "I take that as a very high compliment, Lila Mae. And if you don't get cracking on it, I'm going to remind you about those very words again and again till you do."

With that, he stepped back and gave her a little wave as he set out again on his walk. By now, it was dusk, and the shadow cast by the Old Courthouse made the park even darker. It wasn't long before all she could see of him was the glowing ember of his cigar. Then he turned the corner, and he was gone.

On the way home, though it wasn't strictly on her way, she spun by Midas Muffler. It was well after eight, and she really wasn't expecting to see Wellesley's car or the van. She didn't. But somehow merely going by the place where he worked gave her a kind of thrill, the knowledge he had been there earlier and would be there tomorrow. If only he would call, maybe, just maybe, she could give him a second chance. It wouldn't be easy, and if he stepped out of line one more time, that would be it. But perhaps she had been harsh. Perhaps she had been judgmental. She sighed. There was a real battle going on there inside her between head and heart, some as yet unthought-of carnival ride full of peaks and dips and whirls that left her dizzy as a dust demon. With sinking, leaping exhilaration, she let the notion take hold of her.

There was no doubt about it.

She was in love.

"Lila Mae?" Eliot's head popped through the door as Lila Mae was dressing Miss Johnson. "Have you got any draw-sheets left on your cart?"

At the sight of him, Miss Johnson let out a theatrical and studied "Eek," which didn't really surprise Lila Mae, who had endured a single session at the Johnson Academy for Young Women years and years before, where she had been sent to learn table manners and how to write thank-you notes.

"Oh, stop," she scolded. "Eliot doesn't have the slightest interest in you, believe me."

"And never would have," Eliot added, picking up one of the linens he needed.

"You stop too, Eliot. You could have at least knocked."

"Yes, ma'am," he piped mischievously, and was on his way.

She allowed herself a smile. She had awakened this morning feeling strangely chipper, with the sense somehow that the tide had turned. There was really no good explanation for it, but after hitting rock bottom with the Frank Meachum incident, she just felt things in general had begun to assume some sort of shape, though she was hard pressed to describe precisely what they resembled. It was sort of like lying on your back on a summer's day and watching a thunderstorm build, trying to see what the clouds most looked like. Of course, that particular parallel wasn't probably the best one to have come to mind.

As she was on her way to start the men, Nurse Palmer gestured her over. "Lila Mae, Wendy just called in sick. Could you stay on through swing tonight? As soon as they've got everybody down after dinner you can go. But if we're short, it takes forever to get through it."

She did not relish the notion of a double shift. She had never worked one before, but had heard the horror stories out of Priscilla and Billie Jean. If eight hours was enough to tire anybody out, twelve or fifteen was cruel and unusual punishment. Still, Nurse Palmer was asking her, and Lila Mae felt a little proud, as if this was a sign she was finally accepted, had finally earned enough trust and competence that they would come to her when they needed a helping hand.

"Sure," she said. "Sure, I can stay, I guess."

"You'll be out of here by nine," Nurse Palmer said, as Lila Mae continued down the hall. "Count on it."

She answered the page for Number 34, where Ellie Breckenridge was looking for her old iron skillet to fry up some corn mush, and was not pleased at Lila Mae's suggestion that she probably left it in Galveston fifty years ago. In the hallway, Mrs. Perkins was whining for another blanket. On her way to the linen closet, Lila Mae noted Billie Jean and Priscilla deep in conference by the kitchen door. As she approached, Billie Jean gestured her over conspiratorially.

"Good news, honey," she said. "Consuela says Lee's finally quit."

Lila Mae raised her eyebrows. "That's good news?"

"Darn tootin'," Priscilla snapped. "For you and Eliot anyway. No more runs and a half. They'll have to hire somebody new to replace him, and that means you won't have to do the men anymore."

Lila Mae knew she should be pleased, though, frankly, she had gotten so accustomed to the extra work it hardly fazed her anymore. But, more than that, she thought of losing all those patients, Mr. Meachum and Mr. McNeely, and Mr. Ricks, of course.

She shrugged. "Well, they really aren't that much trouble. I'll kind of miss them."

"Miss them all you want," Priscilla said. "You'll get paid just as much for that as you got paid for taking care of them."

Billie Jean shook her head. "We should have had a temp in here the day after Lee hurt himself. I can never believe how cheap this place can be."

Glancing over Priscilla's shoulder, Lila Mae noticed the page light blinking over 33. She couldn't imagine what on earth Alice Fitzer wanted. Usually, once she was up and about, she pretty well took care of herself. Lila Mae took off, squeezing between the wheelchairs of Mr. Gumbal and Mrs. Limerick, newly back from St. Justin's and twice as ornery as before, as they confronted each other in a Mexican standoff in the middle of the corridor.

Coming up the hallway, she could hear Alice's voice, and picked up her pace as her scalp began to tingle. Something was wrong. By the time she reached the door, she was running.

At first, she thought it was merely that Alice was hung up on a blanket. Her wheelchair was tangled in that afghan she always dragged around with her and she was trying to disengage it, straining to get the wheels moving. But then she heard her, at the same instant she saw the look on her face.

"Lila! Lila!" Alice gestured to her fiercely. "Lila! She's drowning! Drowning!"

Lila Mae felt the panic even before she glanced over at the other bed, or heard the wheezing that grew more and more desperate as the two hands stabbed the air, seeking somehow to fall at that wrinkled throat. Mrs. Voxburg was flailing under the sheets, already slightly blue, even from a distance. Lila Mae froze in the doorway.

"Drowning! She's downing!" Alice wailed.

"Eliot! Eliot!" It was her own voice echoing down the corridor. "Eliot!"

She saw him appear, first walking, then running toward her. "Eliot!"

He was at the intersection of the halls, near the nurses' station.

"Get Nurse Palmer! It's Mrs. Voxburg. Hurry!"

He vanished from her field of vision. She stumbled into the room. "It's all right, Alice." But it was not all right. Mrs. Voxburg was ever wilder. Lila Mae pushed on across the room, which in that instant felt infinitely large. "Mrs. Voxburg! Mrs. Voxburg!" She was beside her, looking down into those starting eyes, the hands now clawing at that wrinkled turkey throat. "It'll be all right, Mrs. Voxburg, it'll be . . ."

Eliot slammed through the door with Nurse Palmer in hot pursuit.

"Get the aspirator! Quick!"

Then Eliot was gone.

Nurse Palmer pushed Lila Mae roughly aside and had her hand down Mrs. Voxburg's throat in the blink of an eye, probing for an obstruction, trying to open the way for air. Suddenly, Eliot was back with the machine on squeaky wheels, and Nurse Palmer took the tube and shoved it into Mrs. Voxburg's mouth and there was an obscene sucking sound as the pump began to pound and the clear chamber of what looked to Lila Mae like an old vacuum began to fill with soft green mucus. It went on and on and Nurse Palmer wrenched the tube ever deeper and that ugly, nasty noise grew louder and Lila Mae was feeling a little faint as Eliot hung near, waiting for instructions, his eyes bulging with concentration.

"How's her heart?" he bellowed.

Nurse Palmer's left hand shot to Mrs. Voxburg's neck. "Okay. Okay. I think we're okay." She began to withdraw the tube, and Mrs. Voxburg's color shifted subtly from blue to blue-white, and then, very gradually, toward her normal paleness. Slowly, very slowly, the tension in the room dissipated, and Lila Mae felt her breath began to come back again, as Eliot's shoulders and Nurse Palmer's face signed to her that the crisis had passed.

Mrs. Voxburg was breathing normally, at least for her, and the three of them slipped cautiously back from the bed, as if any sudden movement might trigger another attack. Alice Fitzer had her face in her hands, rocking gently in her wheelchair, still stuck in the muddle of the afghan.

"We're okay," Nurse Palmer said, her voice even. "We're okay."

She back-stepped toward the door. "I'm calling her doctor. I want him here this afternoon. I don't like this. . . ." She was gone.

Lila Mae found herself beside Alice, rubbing her back. "It's all right. Didn't you hear Mrs. Palmer? It's going to be all right."

"No," Alice said, her face still hidden. "No. I know it. It's not all right."

"Now, honey . . ."

Eliot motioned Lila out to the corridor. When she at last saw Alice's eyes, she followed him.

"What?"

"Lila Mae," Eliot said soberly, "Lile, I don't think she's going to last. You should be ready for that."

All afternoon, Lila Mae hovered. About one-thirty, Mrs. Voxburg's doctor arrived. He examined her, prescribed nothing new, asked to be advised of any changes. He was a small, neutral man, and Lila Mae, though it pained her, realized he was just as she imagined Mrs. Voxburg's doctor would be, as blasted of history as Mrs. Voxburg herself, readable only in the broadest terms.

Three o'clock came and went. The swing shift arrived, most of whom she didn't know by name. She kept her usual women's run, with one of the two P.M. orderlies, Paul, taking over the men. It was a little odd to see the patients at a different time of day, even though, with most, their conditions didn't allow for much of a change in routine. Still, she was surprised to find Ellie Breckenridge sitting quiet and still, watching the world go by, and Mr. Gumbal, so cranky in the mornings, almost charming to the afternoon staff. She waved at Mr. Ricks a couple times as she passed by his room, where he was working with the physical therapist, flat on his back on the bed as she bent and unbent his leg at the knee.

"Not too much longer and you'll be out of here."

He smiled. "One way or another, I suspect."

Mrs. Voxburg was sleeping. Lila Mae stood by her bed, watching her shallow bird-breaths rising and falling beneath the thin gown. She readjusted the pillows, checked the catheter bag, drew the curtains slightly so there was no light in the old woman's eyes. Alice Fitzer rocked still in her wheelchair across the room, broodingly and uncharacteristically silent, picking at the afghan over her knees.

On break, in a lounge full of strangers, Lila Mae asked, "Do you suppose they've called Mrs. Voxburg's family?"

"Doubt it, honey," said a large black woman, Dottie, according to her name tag. "They don't, usually, till it's all over. People don't like dealing much with what we put up with day to day."

Paul took a large bottle of soda water, marked with an adhesive-tape label, PRIVATE STOCK/HANDS OFF!, out of the refrigerator. "All her family's out of state anyway, I think. Some old man, her brother maybe, used to come to visit her, but he died last year. One of her kids was here once, but she lived in Houston or something."

Lila Mae shuddered. "Do you think," she said in a thin voice, "do you think she'll make it through the night?"

Dottie shrugged. "Can't tell. Sometimes they surprise you. But Mrs. Voxburg doesn't look like she's one for much funning around."

After nine o'clock, a peculiar peace descended on Quiet Meadows, one Lila Mae hadn't expected. It was different from that deadly silence at 6:00 A.M., broken only now and then by a vague whimper, and after that dashed entirely by the clang and clatter of breakfast. Now, with more than half the patients down, there was time for more than quick chitchat with those who were still up and about. In the parlor, the television was on, and Mr. Gumbal, Mr. Pope, Mrs. McNulty, and Billy McNeely were playing some sort of game with a spinner and a complicated board. As long as there were no cards or dice, Lila Mae concluded, it passed muster as a game free of gambling, though she noted Billy McNeely had a bulging pocketful of change, and wondered if he was betting his nickels on the outcome of the contest.

Nurse Wheeler noticed Lila Mae as she passed the nurses' station.

"You can go on home, Lila Mae. I think we're okay now. Thanks for helping out."

"I've got a couple more things to finish up, and then I'll be on my way," Lila Mae said. She walked back to the service entrance and clocked out: 9:48. Then, no longer on company time, she crept down the corridor to 33.

Alice was sleeping, stretched out on her back, snoring softly with her mouth gaping. They had her posied, which sounded so pleasant—like hollyhocked or daffodiled—until you realized that what it meant was tied down. Alice had a tendency to wake up in the night and forget that her legs didn't work anymore. Quiet Meadows did not need her breaking a hip as she tried to toddle off to the bathroom on her own.

Lila Mae pushed the door to and tiptoed across the room. Her sight slowly adjusted to the darkness, and she could see Mrs. Voxburg's face, her eyes open, staring toward the ceiling. Lila Mae pulled a chair next to the bed and sat down. She reached under the covers, drew out one of Mrs. Voxburg's hands, and held it in her own.

There in that dim room, she lost track of time. Alice had an alarm clock, but Lila Mae's view was blocked by the guards on the bed. Occasionally, she would hear someone pass by in the corridor, but, for the next hour or so, no one thought to enter. She might have even dozed a little. Her mind was peculiarly blank. None of her problems, at this moment, seemed to have any weight at all, gauzy, silly things beside the brute fact of Mrs. Voxburg's flickering, flickering like a spent flame.

When the door finally did open, it was Stewart, coming on at eleven.

"Lila Mae?" he said, his warm chocolate face looming out of the black. "Lila Mae, what are you doing here?"

She looked at him serenely. "I'm just sitting with her. I clocked out. She doesn't have anybody in the world, so I thought I'd stay with her a bit."

He looked at her, both quizzical and kind. "Well, I don't know what Phillips is going to say, but I guess it's all right. If she needs anything, let me know. The aspirator's down in Shroeder's room right now. If she has another crisis, yell for me and then go get it."

He left.

"I'm here, Mrs. Voxburg. I'm here. Lila Mae," she whispered. That was all. And perhaps it would have been better not to give her a name. Just let her imagine whoever she wished: her dead brother or her daughter in Houston or her momma, or Mr. Voxburg or some friend from her girlhood, or maybe that secret love Lila Mae had once conjured for her who had been her Wellesley Coe. At the end, our comfort should come from whom we most would wish, and Lila Mae now thought of herself not as one of the day aides at Quiet Meadows, not even as Lila Mae Bower Pietrowsky from Rhymers Creek, but, even if it were blasphemous, a little like an angel, a good spirit of this world who would hold this old woman's hand until it was taken by the good spirit of the next.

> Hush, little baby, don't say a word,
> Papa's gonna buy you a mockingbird.
> If that mockingbird don't sing,
> Papa's gonna buy you a diamond ring.

Lila Mae's voice was soft, barely audible, and she moved back and forth in the chair almost imperceptibly, very slowly. It was a silly song, really, and she didn't know the right words, but she sang those that came to her, and magically, inexplicably, verse after verse poured from her lips.

> If that diamond ring don't shine,
> Papa's gonna buy you a valentine.

As she went along, she thought she sometimes heard a low humming, a vague, breathless attempt to mimic her, to follow along. She stopped singing for an instant, brimming with the hope that Mrs. Voxburg was not worse but better, that she had again found that place in her mind where she had misplaced her speech. But in the silence, she realized the sound came not from beside her but from the other bed.

"Alice?" she whispered.

Alice Fitzer did not answer, but only continued with the melody, ghostly, sad, and Lila began again.

> If that brand-new bike gets broke,
> Papa's gonna buy you a case of Coke.
>   If that case of Coke turns flat,
> Papa's gonna buy you a ball and bat.

It went on and on, a whole infinite list of simple desires, silly ones with silly rhymes, but Lila Mae now could not stop, as if that song were some kind of spell, some magical chant that would keep death at bay as long as she had voice.

> If you go and lose one glove,
> Papa's gonna find you a man to love.
>   If that man don't suit just fine,
> Papa's gonna send you the next in line.

The point was that Mrs. Voxburg was not alone, not that Lila Mae was there, but that someone was, though Lila Mae, perhaps, was not a bad choice, or so she thought, because in these last months she had come to know alone, as much as one can know it in thirty years or so, and it had given her, at least, the wisdom of experience, and the determination that Mrs. Voxburg, this woman she had met after she had almost ceased to be a woman at all, would not be left bereft and solitary in the end.

> If that Ferris wheel won't turn . . .

Suddenly, Mrs. Voxburg grabbed Lila Mae's fingers hard, and an unnatural, ratcheting sound issued out of her, a noise unlike any Lila Mae had ever heard. The old woman began to tremble violently, starting up off the mattress. Her grip tightened fiercely. Lila Mae wrenched her hand away and bolted out of the chair.

"Stewart! Stewart!" She plunged into the hall, running toward Mr. Shroeder's room. "Stewart!"

"Get the aspirator, Lila Mae!" she heard him shout from behind her, as Nurse Phillips dashed by. She whirled into 17 and wrestled the clanking castered machine down the hall. In the room, Nurse Phillips and Stewart were starting CPR, the nurse rhythmically breathing in and then blowing down that wrinkled old throat as Stewart smashed his bunched fists on that fragile breast time after time, as if he could beat Mrs. Voxburg to life again. Lila Mae froze next to the machine, watching, paralyzed.

She knew she should be doing something, but for an instant it did not come to her. Then she heard it, as from a great distance: "Pray. Pray!" But, even then, the words did not come, those formulas, those polite requests, even those thundering entreaties the preachers on SBC could deliver in the face of any perceived emergency of the body or spirit. And what should she pray for? That Mrs. Voxburg remain with them, speechless, frightened, some peculiar semblance of the woman she once had been?

Nurse Phillips and Stewart continued with their breathing and battering, more desperate by the second, as Lila Mae's lips moved, imperceptibly. She wished she could make them quit. She understood suddenly what that trembling had been. It was the touch of the other spirit. It was the touch of the angel. In the barest whisper, she did not pray. There was no need. Softly, her tongue made the words: "Go. Go now. It's all right, Mrs. Voxburg. Go now."

Nurse Phillips stopped.

She released her pinch on Mrs. Voxburg's nose and extended an arm toward Stewart, touching his shoulder. Sweat was streaming down his face and arms, shining on his dark skin in the soft light of the bed lamp. He slammed his fists down one final time and then stepped away. He was breathing like he had run a mile, and it was a moment before he could stand straight. Nurse Phillips leaned forward again and gently closed Mrs. Voxburg's eyes.

"I'll call her doctor," she said, and walked out.

Stewart turned to Lila Mae, still rooted in the same spot, the aspirator next to her.

"Lila Mae, I'm sorry. I'm sorry. She's gone."

She might have left then. There was no more to be done. Nurse Phillips, when she came back with a sedative for Alice Fitzer, told her to go on home. But, sunk in the chair next to the body, she still could not bring herself to abandon Mrs. Voxburg. Stewart came in with a fresh gown and linens.

"I've got to dress her now, Lila Mae, before the guy from the funeral home gets here."

"I'll do it," Lila Mae said flatly, tonelessly. She stood up and took the clean-smelling bedclothes and gown from Stewart. Then he left.

She went into the bathroom, and came back with a wash-cloth, slightly damp. She pulled off the old gown and gently, one last time, washed that shrunken, twisted body, now, for these moments anyway, limp and malleable beneath her touch. Like those all through time, she bathed the dead; like Joseph of Arimathea, like the humblest farm girl in India or Peru, she made ready those mortal remains for the rituals of burial. When the dressing was done, she turned the body this way and that, so the bed now a bier would bear no sign of that last relaxation, of that final release of all the bodily products that had no purpose anymore. She stepped back, her arms folded, suddenly very cold, looking down on the body till Stewart came in again.

"We have to move the bed down to the supply closet," he whispered. "The mortician will pick it up there. They don't want the body kept in the room any longer than necessary. One of the patients might notice."

The absurdity of it did not strike her then. She helped him roll the bed away from the wall, and together they maneuvered it out the door and down the hall. Nurse Phillips rushed by, already preoccupied with some new emergency.

"For God's sake, cover up her face," she snapped.

Lila Mae bit her lip, leaned over the head of the bed, and slipped the sheet up.

Mrs. Voxburg disappeared.

"You should get some rest, Lila Mae," Stewart said as they closed the door of the supply closet. "You've had a long day."

"Yes." She nodded. "I'll go now."

She got her purse out of 33, an empty space where, as far as she knew, Mrs. Voxburg had always been. Alice Fitzer was snoring again in drugged sleep. Lila Mae headed for the door to the parking lot.

She had forgotten to check to see what time it was: two o'clock? three? It was almost nice out: a warm, starry night, filled with a deep, sleepy quiet that soothed her. Her body was numb, which was probably for the best, because if she gave in to her tiredness, she knew, she would simply curl up in the backseat of her little car and be done with it. She was not sure what she felt: sadness and relief and emptiness and peace all at once. She had thought from time to time that evening, as against her will she considered how things were likely to come out, that she would cry. But she was dry-eyed, and felt no tears lurking there in her breast, threatening at any instant to burst forth.

She reached the car and, for a moment, simply leaned against the door, relishing the night, letting the little breeze cool her forehead and ripple, ever so gently, her hair. The image of Wellesley drifted through her mind, vague as that breath of wind.

She heard footsteps.

"Hi."

"Eliot?" she said as the figure drew closer. "What are you doing here?"

"Stewart called to tell me you were still here when he came on. I told him to get back to me if anything happened." He rested one elbow on the roof of the car. "You okay?"

"Oh, yes, yes," she said softly. "Sleepy. But everything's taken care of now. Everything's over."

The two of them stared into the night for a moment, silent. Then Lila Mae said, "For her, it was probably a . . ."

". . . blessing," Eliot finished for her, then smiled. "It probably was, Lila Mae, in her case."

"You know"—she cocked her head pensively—"even so, sometimes, sometimes it just seems so unfair, to me."

"What?"

"Death. Or maybe not death, but how people die. Why can't people just go to sleep and never wake up. Enjoy life, get old, have all the fun they can, and then suddenly it's over. That's what I mean. Not fair."

"I guess not," Eliot said, "but at least Mrs. Voxburg had her chance to give a whole lot of things a try before she got dealt a bum hand. I know people these days who have just barely got started and then they're gone."

Of course, she thought, though with no shadow of judgment at this late hour, there's that new disease. "You're right. At least she had that." She touched his arm. "It must be hard for you. To lose friends like that."

"It's not that many, in these parts, anyhow. Not yet . . ." He looked up into the sky. "But it does make you realize how fragile it all is. How tomorrow or the next day or the day after that, it could all be gone, and you're on your way someplace else or maybe nowhere at all."

"Oh, no," Lila Mae said with quiet assurance. "To someplace else, Eliot. There's a someplace else sure as we're standing here."

He laughed softly. "If you say so, Lile. You sure you're okay?"

"I'm fine, Eliot. Go on home. The both of us have to be up in a couple hours."

"Yeah, we'll be a fine pair tomorrow." He lumbered up straight and stepped away. "You drive careful," he said.

"You, too. Eliot?"

He stopped and turned to face her.

"Thank you," she said.

"No trouble, Lile." He started walking again. "No trouble at all."

It was a moment more before she heard the roar of his infernal machine. It split the night like the outbreak of war, and she shook her head, wondering how many of the patients had just shot bolt upright in their beds. She listened until it was a mere purr in the distance. Then it was silent.

She got in the car and let the engine idle briefly, thinking that, despite all that had happened, despite her loss of faith in "World of Love," she had meant what she had just said about that someplace else, that better place. She still felt certain, deep in her heart, that Mrs. Voxburg was on her way to that eternal house party where everybody you ever liked was there. This night, however, there was something new, for Lila Mae had begun to wonder if there might be an invitation outstanding for Eliot as well.

Even before the alarm went off, the phone rang. The jangling pulled Lila Mae from what she thought must be a drunken sleep, though she had never really had one of those. Her eyes simply refused to open at first, as she groped her way into the living room to still the racket of the bell. She found the phone on the far side of the La-Z-Boy.

"Hello? . . . Momma? . . . Momma, why on earth are you calling now? I worked extra shifts. I've hardly had any sleep. . . . What? . . . What!"

She was suddenly wide awake, her mouth gaping in shock, and then, almost immediately, her muscles loosened and she sank into the lounger.

"Oh, Momma, don't tell me that. . . . It's not what I need to hear, Momma. It's not what I need to hear at all. . . ."

FIVE

The death of LaVonne Jackson proved the fatal blow to the "World of Love" ministry. Since Lila Mae had abandoned her usual eight o'clock date with Ted and Becky, things had grown exponentially worse. From what she picked up from the papers that morning, Lila Mae learned that Becky had been so heavily sedated during one show she had slid off her chair onto the floor in a dead faint, while Ted had grown so distraught that not only was he suffering a virtually constant and vicious colitis, but also regularly firing and then rehiring people hour to hour, only to turn around next day and send the same heads rolling once again. In the staff meetings, he had apparently taken to talking a great deal about survivalism and Jim Jones, which understandably set most of the staff on edge. He was determined to find the traitors in the midst of the "World of Love" he had created, and, in private audiences, browbeat cast members, singers, assistant pastors, cameramen, prop mistresses, makeup artists, best boys, and key grips with Stalinist determination. Despite the inevitable speculation, it appeared that LaVonne's suicide resulted from one such session too many, during which she was accused of all manner of Satanic associations, rather than from her having been one of Ted's "special" girls on the staff, his tastes running to blondes and especially, redheads. As Lila Mae thought about it, she realized there had been an inordinate number of carrot-tops attached to "World of Love," far out of proportion to their numbers in the general population.

LaVonne's suicide note, a neatly typed confession to all manner of activities so base and treacherous that it was immediately released by World of Love World Headquarters, was almost as quickly exposed as a fraud, most likely concocted in the inner sanctum of Holy Pines, Ted's and Becky's palatial residence at Hilton Head. As best as could be determined from other WOL Singers, in whom LaVonne had confided, and some garbled phone calls to her family in Newark the night of her death, she had simply been overwhelmed by despair at the revelations regarding the ministry to which she had devoted herself for the past four years. From the very beginning, she had been medicated, and finally, on her last night, had driven to a liquor store just down the road from SBC studios and purchased two liters of gin. In tandem, the pills and liquor had made short work of her.

Lila Mae was devastated. She called in sick to work, guiltily, but was unable to get any more sleep than the two or three hours she had caught the night before. First Mrs. Voxburg, now this. It was almost too much to bear. She wished she had

had a VCR, so she might have taped some of LaVonne's singing off earlier broadcasts, and wondered if a memorial record and tape would be released. She remembered that evening LaVonne had sung "Bride of Jesus," and it brought tears to her eyes to recall how that voice could transport her back to those days in her life when everything seemed so wonderfully simple. Her heart went out to LaVonne, who, far more than she or even Momma, really had looked for care and solace and truth and certainty in "World of Love," and had instead suffered a betrayal so terrible she had been driven to commit what she must have known was about the most terrible sin imaginable.

That raised, for Lila Mae, a difficult and probably insoluble question: What was God to do with LaVonne? As she understood it, Scripture was pretty clear when it came to suicide, and yet, would He really hold LaVonne to such strict rules when she was obviously out of her head with loss and grief? Then again, no one, it seemed to Lila Mae, would ever take his own life lightly, and if that were the case, God would have a modicum of sympathy, at least, for every self-slaughterer who knocked on the Pearly Gates.

It gave her a headache, as theology always did, but she could not bring herself to believe that God would damn LaVonne for a momentary and terrible weakness. Surely, in addition to being a strict and unmovable judge, He was also entirely aware of the frailty, not merely of the flesh, but of the spirit, and would somehow find a way to pardon a crime whose only victim was the desperate LaVonne herself.

With a perverse rage, she awaited 8:00 P.M. Lila Mae was not even sure the program would be aired as scheduled. She watched Dan Rather, gorging herself on the most recent revelations, at every moment more hurt, more angry, more overwhelmed. It was not merely LaVonne, she realized. She had achieved last night, at the bedside of a dying old woman, a new kind of peace with the way of the world, and Ted and Becky Standish had done their very best to ruin it all.

As the show began, the choir appeared in black, or at least part of it. There were a number of absent members, and indeed, in the audience as well there seemed to be a vacant seat here and there. The theme had finally acquired that dirgelike pace Lila Mae had once predicted, and, needless to say, there was no sign of Becky. As the music ended, Ted appeared, microphone in hand; his, the face of a drowning man. His eyes were wide, and he had something very close to a tic, which kept twisting the left side of his mouth.

"As you know, friends and partners, we here at 'World of Love' have suffered a devastating loss, a loss that can hardly be expressed. Our dear LaVonne, LaVonne Jackson, is no longer with us, taken from us by her own hand. . . ."

Lila Mae could hardly look at him, his handsomeness now a mask for some unimaginable creature beneath. She could not help thinking of *Peter Pan*—was it?—with the crocodile who cried salt tears as he plotted and planned his next meal?

Ted kept talking, his voice strained with emotion, mourning the passing of such a vital member of the "World of Love" family. Again, Lila Mae fought for control, for what had this family brought over the airways turned out to be? No family at all. Whatever their faults, Momma and Fred, Lonnie and Cindy, even little Joey out in Oregon, certainly meant more to her, could be counted on by her. Even the staff at Quiet Meadows, people she had known mere weeks, cared and demanded care like family, not like the easy bunch there in Charleston, South Carolina, who, when it came down to it, were primarily interested in how much of your monthly paycheck you might be shipping their way to keep the airplane fueled for that trip to the Holy Land and the satellite bills paid. Certainly, LaVonne had found no solace in that bosom.

The camera pulled to a tight close-up. Ted Standish loomed into Lila Mae's living room, twitching, sweaty. She shuddered. It was almost like looking into the maw of the Beast.

"Now this is hard, my friends. Hard to tell you. Hard to discuss. But I am clay. Clay! Just as we all are, mortal vessels subject to be filled with temptation. And I . . ." His lip quivered. "I . . ." And again. "I have sinned. Sinned! Sinned grievously against all of you. Against my most dear wife, Becky, who is so shattered she cannot be with us here tonight. Against my Lord. Oh, the Devil had me by the throat. I could not resist him with his sweet words and promises, his invitations to earthly pleasures and earthly glory. And I too must beg forgiveness, of Becky, of you, most of all, of God."

Lila Mae shifted in her chair. This kind of confession made her uncomfortable, for it made her feel oddly unworthy. She knew in her heart she should forgive, and that was what Ted was asking for, the forgiveness of each and every member of his flock. She had been through this before a few months ago with another evangelist, and she had been moved, she would admit, by what she perceived as the fall of a great man, the public penance of someone who had set himself up as a leader for us all, had acted as judge and prophet, and then had been revealed as poor and naked as the rest. His weeping had touched her, his vows of reform. Three months later he had been back in the pulpit again. This time, she steeled herself. She would not be so easily taken in.

"It is hard to speak of my sins . . ."

Though it had been so easy, she thought, for him to speak of his virtues.

"... and though they are heavy, I know you will forgive me."

And had he forgiven the ones who had not listened? The ones he railed against as the agents of the Devil? The different ones? The ones who saw things in another way? The ones who, for one reason or another, he had decided to dislike?

"The details are unimportant. . . ."

As Abner Halliday's had been? How often, Lila Mae wondered, had she and all the rest in that vast and speechless audience savored the politely expressed but sordid mess that others had made of their lives, point by point, outlined in bold strokes so that each and every one might fill in the specifics according to his own dark imaginings? No, from Ted she wanted details, which ones of those newspaper stories were true, which ones elaborations? Lila Mae wanted to know the story of the corruption of a once-virtuous man, a man who, she still at least wished, had been filled with a mission, had once believed in that specialness of every human soul.

The tears now streamed down Ted's face without shame, and he raised his arms to Heaven. "Forgive, please forgive me, who has transgressed, who has lost his way, who has malatani moloki wantsa moerreri, polkatsi lundo morani setti, alanno. . . ."

Lila Mae covered her ears. The sins to be spoken in tongues? Sins to remain nameless? But what if there were names for them: lust and avarice and covetousness and pride. Pride, above all. That was the one sin, she realized, which eclipsed all others, the one sin that was perhaps unforgivable. The sin of Satan, after all, the sin of which those who preached the Word, in their railings against all other lapses, somehow never managed to quite address.

"All I can do is ask that you forgive me my failings"—he was back to English again—"and welcome me, chastened, once again in fellowship into your home. We have traveled a long road together. Your prayers, your hope, your dollars have made 'World of Love' what it is. We must not lose what we have made. If I have been weak, amen, so be it, but we must keep working, keep building this ministry with every ounce of our strength, every dime we can spare. Remember, my friends, what it tells us in the Gospel of Matthew, chapter seven, first verse: 'Judge not that ye be not judged. . . .' "

Lila Mae did not anticipate it. She did not know where she found the strength. All she heard was that echo of Wellesley Coe weeks ago, from the mouth of the very man who had given her, in that moment, such proud assurance of her own virtue. Her palm was suddenly around the telephone table, and as the phone itself crashed to the floor, the round, marble-topped stand she had bought on a whim the week of the divorce at Woolworth's flew through the air as if it had wings of its own and shattered Ted Standish's face into a shower of glass and sparks and confused transistors. There was a huge noise of air rushing into a vacuum, as if Ted himself had suddenly been swallowed in the infinite bell of eternity.

A little after nine o'clock, after she had put the sweeper away, after she had thrown the circuit breaker to pull the plug of the ruined Motorola that had been hers and Eddie's and that she would now have to replace for some unconscionable sum of money, she called Momma. The phone rang once, twice, three times. Lila Mae paid limited attention, her mind on the satisfaction that busting that television had given her, even if it was going to mean at least couple of weeks' pay to get a new one. Six times, seven. A new sense of a clean break filled her, the thrill of having come to some of her own conclusions, or having the courage to do something not because someone else told her to do it, but because she trusted her own heart and mind. Twelve. Thirteen . . .

What was wrong here? Momma never let the phone ring so long. Usually, she pounced on it before the third jangle, and there had been times when Lila Mae had not even realized it had sounded at the other end before she heard her mother's voice. Surely she hadn't gone out, and there had been no mention of Fred's or Lonnie's planning to stop by to take her anyplace.

Suddenly, Lila Mae felt a wave of dread. LaVonne's death, Ted's performance tonight: They might just have sent Momma over the edge. Before she had really thought it out consciously, she had her keys in her hand and was headed out the door.

It was not a long trip to Momma's. No trip within the limits of Rhymers Creek was very long, even these days. She was off the seat and had both feet on the driveway before she remembered to lean back and cut the engine, then set off running toward the gate and up the front walk.

This was the house. Her house. The place that still, when she spoke about home not as where she slept but where her soul lived, she was talking about. It was hard, at her age, not to have four walls that had at least begun to replace in knowledge and affection the plain, clean clapboards of this bungalow with what had been her bedroom in the back, the boys together in the vast room under the eaves. With Eddie, there had been a series of apartments and finally the little house on Allison Street where that note ended up taped to the table. And now, the half of a duplex to call her own seemed just a resting place, an extended motel room until she put her life back together and moved on.

She darted up the steps and across the porch, reaching for the doorknob as if she had never left home, bursting full into the living room, a feature of the house that Momma had always detested.

"Hello, dear."

Her mother glanced up at her, nonplussed, from the divan, where she was barricaded with pillows, facing the tube.

"Momma! Momma, are you all right?" Lila Mae managed to gasp out.

Her mother's face creased with vague annoyance. "Of course I'm all right. Why shouldn't I be all right?"

"I tried to call," Lila Mae said. "I called about fifteen minutes ago and you didn't answer and I thought maybe there was something wrong."

"Well, when I didn't hear from you," Momma said, "I decided to unplug the phone so I could watch this program in peace. So why don't you pull up a chair and be quiet."

Lila Mae did as she was told, as she always did in this house, though not, as was also common, with the best of grace. Momma had the set tuned to one of the UHF channels that Lila Mae had never been able to get good reception on. There was a woman seated cross-legged on a low stool, talking in a voice that reminded Lila Mae of the one Norma had recently affected.

"Momma, what on earth is this?"

Her mother gave her a lazy gesture of dismissal. "It's called channeling, Lila Mae. Heavens! Don't you know anything? Monkra, he's a man from 20,000 B.C., he's talking through Trudy there. He's so wise, it's amazing."

Lila Mae leaned closer, still not quite clear on what it was she was supposed to see. A nice-looking, middle-aged woman—one trying to look not quite as old as she obviously was—was speaking in a sort of basso-profundo chant, slowly and rhythmically, her eyes tightly closed and her posture similar to that Lila Mae had once seen in a photo of Sumo wrestlers in Japan. She squatted on that stool and was grunting something about the seventh root race that was evolving in Southern California, the place where, Lila Mae nastily suspected, this woman had her zip code.

"Momma," she said slowly, "Momma, I cannot, can not, believe you are watching this."

Her mother scowled, "Oh, Lila Mae . . . Now of course, at first, I was a little worried it was occult, but then there was a minister on one of the shows who said that John ,the Baptist was probably channeling, and who talked about the Pentecost and tongues and all that and it's really not all that different, is it?"

Lila Mae didn't reply. Well, was it? After all that had happened, she really didn't know that she could say.

"What about Ted and Becky?"

"Humph!" Momma grunted. "I gave up on them long ago. A couple of snake-oil salesmen, far as I'm concerned."

The blood rushed to Lila Mae's face. "What do you mean?"

"Why do you think I was always changing the subject when you talked about them? I'd read the preview in 'Today's TV' and catch the first five minutes just to make sure they hadn't lied about what they were going to talk about. But really, they were just the limit."

"What are you saying?"

Her mother shrugged. "Well, honey, it seemed so important

to you. I followed it for a while at first, and then again when this scandal was coming out, I wanted to see what they had to say. But, frankly, I got bored real fast. Oh, watch this . . ."

Monkra had apparently tired of delivering the wisdom of 22,000 years ago to the television audience, and Trudy was suddenly shaking like one of those people loosening up for aerobics as Monkra set off to communicate with somebody else in some other time warp.

"Too bad!" Momma said. "He was getting into some really interesting stuff about earthquakes up in Missouri."

Lila Mae burst out of her chair and smacked the button on the television. "Momma," she said, "we have to talk."

"What about?" She was there curled on the davenport like, somehow, in Lila Mae's mind, she always was. Superior. In control. It was that nasty thing women were taught: how to make other people feel like they'd . . . they'd screwed up, that they were putting you out, wasting your time, ruining your fun. There was a poutiness about it, childlike and yet self-consciously manipulative. She had seen Momma use it with her, with Daddy, especially with Fred. It was a pose she herself had used with Eddie, maybe with other people as well, and she hated it.

"Are you telling me, Momma, that you didn't give a damn about Ted and Becky?"

Her mother shook her head. "No, honey, not at all. They did some real good for me, I think, at first. In a lot of ways, they were more laid back than a lot of those preachers on SBC. But then, I just kind of lost patience with them. Too syrupy for my tastes. And all they talked about was money. Now I was willing to see them up to a certain amount, you know that. I made that pledge because I really did want to help them out. But it did get to be a thing with them. I really couldn't see how Jesus could care too much about them, greedy like that. But you seemed so stuck on the show, and, after all, it gave us something to talk about, so I figured, what the hell, if that's how she's getting through the divorce, I can deal with it."

Momma had obviously been watching too many programs originating in Los Angeles. Lila Mae took a deep breath. "Momma. Momma, I've got to tell you something. If I were not the good, Christian woman that you taught me to be, that the Baptist Church made me, that SBC encouraged, I would wring your neck right now."

Momma seemed unperturbed, gazing at Lila Mae with a satisfied serenity, as if she knew perfectly well her neck was in no peril whatsoever. She sighed loudly. "How's Wellesley?"

Lila Mae exploded. "How should I know? I haven't seen him in weeks! Why are you asking me about Wellesley?"

Momma shrugged. "Who else should I ask you about? Who else have you been seeing? Nobody that I know about."

"What are you saying to me!" It was a sharp, animal sound, something not altogether what she expected or could control. "Momma. Momma!" She was willing her voice steady, no easy task at this moment. "Let's get something straightened out. Right now!" She leaned menacingly toward her mother. "Do you know . . . do you have any idea what it was that Wellesley Coe proposed to me a month or so ago?"

Her mother looked at her with an infuriating tranquillity. "I don't have the vaguest idea."

Lila Mae tensed. It was like years of lying—not exactly lying, but playing safe, playing good, playing like everything was really not all that bad, that different—collapsing in a split second. She was now going to make it clear to the woman who bore her that she too was a woman, a woman of near to thirty years, one with experience in the greater world, one who knew what men were about, what they wanted, what kind of things they might, fairly or unfairly, demand.

"Momma," she said evenly, "Momma, not only did Wellesley want to sleep with me, in that way we say that kind of thing today, but Wellesley actually expected me to have the safes in my purse so there wouldn't be any accidents."

Her mother looked at her steadily, unblinking. "Well, did you have any?"

Lila Mae felt her heart starting out of her chest. "Momma, are you being serious?"

"Well, did you have any or not?"

An unexpected darkness passed over her. She was not sure at all what was happening. She looked at her mother, that good Baptist, that woman who had reared her, and she didn't know her anymore. Or, suddenly, she saw not her mother, but another woman, who would not be astounded at much of anything she had to say. "No, Momma, no. Actually, I didn't have any safes with me. Because, from what you taught me years and years ago, a lady did not carry that sort of thing with her. That, if that topic ever came up, it was the man who was responsible for taking care of it, and, even then, a lady would, at least at first, be shocked and appalled that the subject had arisen."

Momma looked at her wonderingly, and also with the beginnings of a terrific sadness, as if somehow, somewhere, they had lost touch with one another in a terrible and inexplicable way. "I can't imagine what you're talking about, Lila Mae."

"To be simple about it, Momma, I guess I figured that if things didn't work out in the long term and it ever got back to you that I'd bedded down with Wellesley Coe, it would kill you."

Momma shrugged. "It might have."

Lila Mae felt her veins bulging. "Well, what should I have done?"

"How should I know, Lila Mae?" Momma said. "You'd have to decide on your own."

"Well then, I decided I wouldn't kill you by sleeping with Wellesley when he asked me."

Her mother looked at her soberly. "Fine, that's fine with me, Lila Mae. I'm not surprised." She shook her head with a peculiar, despairing satisfaction. "After all, you always were a gutless wonder."

It was a moment she had never known before. Lila Mae, so good, the only girl. Lila Mae, who behaved herself, a born-again Baptist from Rhymers Creek. Not flashy, not special, not outstanding. Merely Lila Mae Bower, following the rules, making Daddy proud and Momma proud by being ordinary, not drawing attention to herself, just like good girls were supposed to do. Let the boys make a mark. Her responsibility was to be discreet, virginal, shocked by the notion she would have a pack of rubbers in her purse.

Lila Mae blew off the sofa.

"What are you telling me! What in God's name are you telling me!" All of a sudden, the blood coursing through her heart was pure ice, and all the years she had spent being what she thought everyone expected her to be seemed lost, wasted.

Momma looked at her quizzically. "I suppose that you ought to make your own life. I certainly can't do it for you." She crossed her arms petulantly. "And, frankly, I'm getting tired of pretending that I can give you some kind of direction. Why don't you just take care of yourself?"

Had there been something at hand, she would have thrown

it. Lila Mae stared murderously at Momma, white-haired and clear-eyed, whom she had been feeling sorry for all these years. She suddenly realized that was part of the problem, that women spent too much time feeling sorry for each other, rather than going and doing what they had to do. Certainly, in all these years, that was the last thing that might have defined her. When she felt her marriage with Eddie was a loss, she should have told him, she should have told Momma, she should have told everyone. She could have made it clear she was willing to make it work and, at the same time, indicate she had no intention of hanging around if it didn't. And if she had the yen to sleep with Wellesley Coe, that was her business—not Momma's, not anybody else's, with the exception, of course, of Wellesley himself, and perhaps God, Who might or might not find the whole circumstance of particular interest in the great scheme of things.

She gathered up her purse and headed for the door.

"Momma, you take very good care, and you listen real hard to what Monkra has to say," she said, seething, "because I am telling you now . . ." An old song from her elementary-school days began to play in her head: "I'm telling you eve-ry day . . ." ". . . that from now on I will not be calling evening to evening to see how you are getting on with your life, because I'm going to be getting on with mine!"

Her mother's face colored with a vague flush of panic, and an old, old voice, a quavering whine that Lila Mae knew too well began: "Now, Lila Mae . . ."

"No Lila Mae this or Lila Mae that," she snapped. "You've got to take care of business on your own, just like me, and if it has to be in Rhymers Creek, so be it, amen! So, you get on with it and I will, too. Good night, Momma!" And she slammed out the door.

As she revved the engine, she really hadn't the vaguest notion where she was headed. North was best, she decided, toward Mockdon, toward where people were less likely to know her. It was eleven, but there were stores open till two along the highway. She had something she needed to pick up.

At work next day she spent the first two hours she was there in a haze. She had arrived five minutes late, and hit her run immediately, without even the time for a morning chat in the lounge. It was only after the breakfast trays were up and she had dressed about half the women that she even felt capable of responding to questions with more than two words. Her exhaustion, along with all that had happened over the last couple of days, made her feel curiously disconnected, as if her feet were not quite planted on the ground, but hovering somewhere just above it.

It was all so different. There were the holes, big and small, in her life, which last week, last month, hadn't been there. The entire panorama of things seemed to have changed, and she was still not quite sure how she would deal with that.

In 33, Alice Fitzer sat silent in her wheelchair. The bed that had been Mrs. Voxburg's was back, of course, made up with fresh linen, the night table and bureau across the room empty, their tops shiny and uncluttered, awaiting the arrival of a new patient. Though there was no practical need to spend much time there, Lila Mae made it a point to dawdle a bit as she picked up Alice's tray.

"How are you getting on today, honey?"

Alice looked at her morosely. She shrugged. "As well as I can," she said, "as well as I can."

"Uh-huh." Lila Mae couldn't quite come up with the right words, the words that would be appropriate to say to an old lady who had just watched the old lady who shared her room die. "That's about all we can ask of you, I guess."

Alice nodded. "You know," she said pensively, "I really didn't know Ethel." It was the first time Lila Mae had heard someone call Mrs. Voxburg by her given name. "By the time she came here she was pretty well gone." Alice shook her head sadly. "But I'm still going to miss her. I really am."

Lila Mae touched that old white head. "We all will, honey. It's funny, since I guess none of us really could get very close to her, but we all will."

Around eleven o'clock, she was sufficiently ahead that she felt she could take a break. Priscilla hadn't come in that day, so Billie Jean and Norma were splitting her run, with the latter apparently taking an early lunch. Hunched over in the corner, eating an apple, her nose in a book, Norma looked almost vulnerable as Lila Mae walked in.

"How are things, Norma?" she asked as she took her sack lunch from the refrigerator.

"Not bad. Too much to do. How about you?"

"Oh, things have been a little rough the last few days." Lila Mae sighed. "A lot of things have ..." She stopped in mid-sentence, her eyes widening. "Ah, Norma, what's that book you're reading?"

"It's called Our Bodies, Our Selves," she said.

It was true. Norma sounded like Norma. Her voice was pitched back where it had been when Lila Mae first arrived, before her conversion, before she broke up with Ricky. Lila Mae's mind was a blur; she wasn't precisely sure how she should deal with this turn of events.

"Well, that sounds interesting," she said cautiously. "What's it about?"

Norma smiled at her. "Oppression. Liberation. Understanding yourself as a woman."

"Uh-huh. Well, that sort of thing can be real important."

"That's for sure." Norma leaned toward her. "You know, Lila Mae, you really ought to have a look at it. You're as much a victim of patriarchal, phallocentric conditioning as anybody I've ever met. You could use a little consciousness-raising."

"Well, yes, I suppose I could." The title did have a vague ring to it, though Lila Mae was afraid perhaps it was merely some how-to book, a sort of *The Joy of Sex* for women only. "Maybe when you're done with it, I can borrow it," she said neutrally. "So, ah, did you have a nice time with Stewart and Eliot the other night?"

"Oh, it was wonderful," Norma said. "It's just a fabulous bar, and they introduced me to some great people."

"How nice." Lila Mae smiled bravely. "I'm glad you all enjoyed yourselves."

"We may go down next week again." Norma's eyes twinkled. "Want to come?"

"No, no, that's okay," Lila Mae said quickly. "I'd just be sort of a stick-in-the-mud."

"Suit yourself." Norma stood and launched her apple core into the trash can. Swish. "I better get back out on the floor."

On her way out, she nearly collided with Eliot. "Lile in here?" he asked her.

Norma gestured behind her as she slipped through the door.

"So, how are you, Lila Mae?" He sat down at the table opposite her.

"Okay," she said, "but ..." She lowered her voice. "But what's happened with Norma?"

Eliot shrugged. "What do you mean?"

"Come on, Eliot. She's not stomping around and she's talking like she used to. Has she decided, ah, that she isn't a lesbian after all? "

"No."

"Oh." Despite herself, Lila Mae couldn't mask her disappointment. Even if she was entering into a brave new world where she was going to start making a lot of judgments for herself, breaking some of the old habits would be hard.

"But on the other hand, she hasn't decided that she is."

Lila Mae looked at the smile growing under the three days' growth he was apparently affecting. "Wait a minute, Eliot, I don't think I'm following this."

"Look, Lila Mae," he said, "we took Norma down because Stewart wanted her to talk to this friend of his, Anita, who runs a women's bookstore with her lover down there in the capital. Norma didn't have a notion what she was talking about, and we figured Anita could kind of get her thinking. I mean, you don't just one day realize you're gay and make your life over. It's a process." He relished the word. "Anita gave Norma a couple of books and told her she could call her any time she wanted some more suggestions, and she gave her the number of some lady at Wilson's who's a union organizer and runs a women's group up there that Norma's going to join."

Lila Mae was still confused. "But, well, who's she going to be dating then?"

Eliot laughed. "Whoever she wants, at least for the time being. The important thing is that she likes whoever it is she's going out with, man or woman, and that whoever it is doesn't give her any shit for simply being who she is."

It was making a certain amount of sense. It was as if Norma was going through a kind of reordering similar in ways to the one Lila Mae herself was facing. It was, she realized, the only thing other than a nun-fascination she had ever felt she had in common with the poor girl.

"So, you and Stewart had this all planned," she said.

"Well, not exactly. I was just pissed as hell at her. But Stewart said that being mad about it didn't do anybody any good, especially Norma, so we cooked this up so she could really get things pieced together right in her own mind."

Lila Mae looked at him across from her, all that intimidating hugeness, the tattooed, earringed likeness of the Devil himself. As she stood up, she leaned over and gave him a little peck on the cheek.

He started, and his hand went to the spot where she had kissed him. "What was that for?"

"Oh, just for you being you." She giggled. "Just for you being you, Eliot."

Driving down Mason Street, she could feel herself tremble a little. She still was not absolutely certain that this was the right thing to do. It was forward, maybe downright unladylike. Precisely the kind of thing she had been taught all her life to avoid, behavior that surely Becky would have advised against, much less the Momma of her girlhood. But, in undertaking it, Lila Mae was following both her heart and her head. It was not just a spontaneous act. After the notion occurred to her, she had turned it over carefully in her mind. Now, nervous though she was, she still knew she could never live with herself if she didn't press ahead.

The rest of the day at Quiet Meadows had passed quickly. Mrs. Lindley had called her in at one point, to Lila Mae's surprise, to inquire, none too subtly and with obvious relief, about the latest changes in Norma. Mrs. Lindley, who went to such luckless pains to appear feminine but efficient, hard-nosed but straight-laced, obviously thought that, in that final category at least, in Lila Mae she had found a soul mate, which was not altogether unreasonable in comparison to the other members of the staff. Up until recently, she would have been right. Nonetheless, Lila Mae tried to place Norma's new self as the logical outcome of a process, as Eliot had put it, and when asked about specifics, simply said she couldn't predict how things might work out, but wasn't it encouraging that Norma was making such progress in understanding herself, which would certainly be reflected in her work? That, of course, was the kind of remark that, however she felt in her heart, Mrs. Lindley had to approve of.

About two-thirty, on her way to chart, she noticed the page light on for 23. She detoured and popped her head in the door. Mr. Meachum was gone, and Mr. Ricks, whom she had helped to dress earlier, was in the chair by the window.

"Did you ring, Mr. Ricks?"

He turned toward her. "Oh, good, honey, it's you. I had Frank flip the page on a couple of minutes ago. Come on in."

"What was it you needed?"

"Just to talk a minute. It looks like I'm going to be checking out this afternoon."

In Lila Mae's stomach, a small emptiness opened up. "What?"

"Well, my doctor was through earlier and he thinks I might as well get on home. No point in me taking up space here. There'll be a visiting nurse coming by to make sure everything's going as well as can be expected. So, I just wanted to thank you for all you've done, Lila Mae. You really have made my time here special."

She did not know precisely what to say. It was wonderful, of course. Simply seeing someone leave Quiet Meadows more or less under his own power should fill her with joy. Yet, too, she could not help but be sad to see him go.

"Well, you know I'll miss you. But you can't be sticking around here just to look out for me." She smiled. "Maybe I can come and visit you sometime."

"Oh, I think you'll probably have better things to do than pass the time of day with me." His eyes twinkled. "After all, there's that young man you've got to get to live up to your expectations."

She was afraid she might have blushed. He really was a forward old coot. "We'll just see about that, Mr. Ricks," she said quickly. "But I want you to promise me you'll take good care of yourself."

"Good as I can, though it won't be as easy as it is with you around." He shrugged. "Why, I'll even have to learn how to take my own showers."

"Shame on you. You'll do that just fine." She stood up.

Mr. Ricks reached behind his chair and pulled out a cane. Then, very slowly, he wobbled to his feet.

"I was saving it as a surprise," he said. "I plan to walk out of here on my own, thank you."

She clapped her hands together, a little thrill passing through her she hadn't expected. Then she walked over to him and gave him a hug. "You bet you will, Mr. Ricks."

As she reached the door, he called to her: "Lila Mae."

She turned.

"Just one other thing I wanted you to know. Now I think

you're pretty aware I'm not too impressed with a lot of this church stuff, and I've given you a pretty hard time about it now and then. But I heard the story about what you did the other night."

Her eyebrows shot up.

"With that lady down in 33, the one who died. I just want you to know that that was one of the most Christian things, in the best sense of the word, I ever heard of." He nodded. "You are a good woman, Lila Mae. A very good woman."

She felt a little choked up. "Why, thank you, Mr. Ricks." She was going to say something else, something that would make what she had done seem less special, something to undermine the compliment. But then, all she did was smile, and say again, "Thank you so very much."

The Camaro was there. Of course it's there, you dippy thing, she said forcefully to herself; where did you expect it to be? She flipped on her turn signal and pulled into Midas Muffler, after a moment's hesitation parking right in front of the office, not sneaking around to the side out of sight as she had first planned. If she was going to do this, she certainly shouldn't be skulking around like a thief in the night. She checked her hair in the rearview mirror—acceptable, if not perfect—and then opened the door and stepped nonchalantly out. Behind the counter in the air-conditioned office, Jackie Pomeroy, of the bootlegging Pomeroys back before the county went wet, was doodling on a legal pad and failing to look very busy. Lila Mae had always thought it a bit unfair that old Doc Pomeroy managed to set his whole family up with franchises from all those ill-gotten gains over the years: Jackie with Midas and Mary with the Orange Julius and Elwood, so the story went, with a Mc-Donald's near Laguna Beach in California.

A little bell tinkled as she walked in.

Jackie glanced up from his squiggles. "Why, Lila Mae," he said. "Haven't seen you in quite a while. What can I do for you?"

She sucked in a deep breath that she hoped he didn't notice. "Oh, nothing, Jackie. I just came by to see if Wellesley was around."

"Sure." Jackie grinned. "Sure, he's right out in the garage. Here"—he got up and pulled up the hinged section of the counter—"just come on through."

She followed him to the door in back, which he pulled open and held for her, bellowing, "Wellesley! Hey, Wellesley! You got some company."

He was over on the far side of the shop, and, at first, above the racket of air drills and throbbing pumps and a revving engine out front, he didn't seem to hear. Jackie waved his arms. "Wellesley!"

She saw him stop work, look in their direction. In a mere fraction of a second, his face read half a dozen ways. First, he was merely curious to see who called. Then he saw her, and a kind of glow passed across his eyes. After that, there were two or three different expressions, as his pleasure struggled with his desire to disguise it. Finally, with a slow grin, he walked over to where they were standing.

"What was it you needed, Jackie?"

Jackie stepped back slightly. "Nothing for me, Wellesley. But Lila Mae asked if you was around." He turned back toward the office. "So I'll let you two get on with it. Just don't drop the soap around this one, Wellesley. She can be a wildcat, so I hear."

Wellesley grunted. "Tell it to that brother of yours, Jackie."

He waited till Jackie had closed the door. "So, Lila Mae, what's up?"

"Well, I was just driving by, and I thought"—through the grease and the sweat, she caught the hint of Vitalis—"now it has been a while since I saw Wellesley last"—and he was right there, not two feet away, loose and lanky, with those beautiful green eyes and that little smile—"so I thought I'd just drop in to see"—and oh, how she had liked him always and if he'd made one teeny-weeny mistake was that any reason to condemn him outright?—"how you were getting along."

He nodded. "Well, that was nice of you, Lila Mae. I'm getting along all right, thanks."

"Oh"—he was not making this any easier—"that's good. Hot as it's been and working out here where there's no air-conditioning"—she was making a gesture, after all, and he must realize that—"it must get awfully uncomfortable."

"Not too bad," he said neutrally, "not too bad, really."

He was playing with her; she just knew it. Or was it that she hoped that was the case? What if he had simply given up on her these last few weeks? Simply decided there was no future with her. She felt a little shudder she hoped was invisible. Maybe he was seeing somebody else.

"Like I said, it had been a while, and I . . ."

"Lila Mae"—he folded his arms slowly over his chest—"Lila Mae, if I remember right, the last time we saw each other you made it pretty clear that you didn't much want me coming round anymore."

She straightened up. "Well, Wellesley, it was just that I thought . . . I mean, there was just a kind of misunderstanding the night . . . When we went out then I . . . I . . ." She sighed deeply. "Oh, Wellesley, I'm sorry. I just got upset, I guess. I mean, I thought you'd treated me like ... well, like somebody you weren't very serious about, and it made me feel hurt." She glanced up at him to see if this was having some effect. His face was impassive. "I'm just not used to those kinds of proposi-tions. You know, I was married for a pretty long time and I just ... well, times have changed, I guess."

He stood there for a long moment, and she could hear herself breathing. She kept trying not to look him in the face, because she was afraid she would tear up if she did. He was so close.

"Lila Mae," he said very soberly, "Lila Mae, something maybe you should know is that I don't make that kind of proposition, like you said, all as often as you seem to think, and when I make it, I make it because I think two grown-up people should have a right to show each other how they feel about each other." He stilled her with a raised palm before she could even begin to speak. "But I've thought about it, and you were right; it wasn't time yet, and I should have thought about how, all these years I've been single, you were a married lady and hadn't been doing that much dating. And especially I shouldn't have thought you'd have come prepared, because that by rights ought to be my department as much as yours, but I just got carried away and it was out my mouth before I'd really put my head in gear. And I respect you for saying no and I understand why you were pissed off about it and if you'll let me, I'd like to take you out to Macaffey's-at-the-Quarry tomorrow night for dinner and we can start all over again."

It came out so quickly there at the end that it took her a minute to realize what he had said. She opened her mouth a couple of times to say something, but no sound emerged.

Finally, she took his hand and leaned forward against his

chest, and felt his fingers, very softly, on the back of her head. She thought she was going to cry, but didn't. She found her voice again.

"Oh, yes," she said. "Yes, Wellesley, I'd like that. Yes."

The first surprise of the evening, he would tell her later, was when she suggested they buy the little bottle of champagne. Not the big one, she insisted, because that might go to her head and she wanted to relish every moment of a night as special as this one. Macaffey's overlooked the gravel pit reclaimed by the parks department, across the yawning hole from the Episcopal church. They really had done a good job with it, she thought, planting trees, sowing wildflowers and grass, trying to put back right what had been ripped out two dozen years before, when Mockdon first boomed. Even if they could not undo the destruction the bulldozers and steam shovels had wrought, they had at least tried to make the place pretty again in a different way, start a slow process so that in fifty years, when nobody ever remembered it looking any different, people would be surprised that this wasn't nature's original design.

Wellesley wore a linen jacket that Lila Mae thought was the most elegant thing she had ever seen on a man. It turned out to have been a birthday present from an old girlfriend that he had never worn before, but that she found out only much, much later. She had a new dress, a very pale peach, which she had picked out at Delaney's within an hour after she left Midas Muffler. She then whirled into Walgreen's and headed for the cosmetics counter.

"Mrs. Rudolph! Thank the Lord you're back." Her relief was boundless as she spotted that familiar gray head behind the counter. "I have to talk to you. I need your undivided attention, because we've got to get this right the first time. . . ."

The process turned out to be so complicated that, at closing time, Lila Mae went back to the store and picked up Mrs. Rudolph with a canvas bag full of samples. For the next two hours, in the kitchen, where the light was best, they conducted a series of experiments with more different face paints and nail polishes and hair stuff and perfumes than Lila Mae had owned in the course of her whole life. By eleven, however, the decisions were made. Both Mrs. Rudolph and Lila Mae were in agreement. Lila Mae did not look pert. She did not look cute. She looked like a woman, and a beautiful one at that.

Next day at work, Eliot teased her for wearing a little net on her head to keep her hair from getting mussed, and Priscilla pestered her every time she saw her. "Well, come on, Lila Mae. Who is it? What's this big production all about?"

In Mrs. Wallerby's room, as Lila Mae picked up the lunch tray, Elmer noticed it as well.

"Somebody must have a big date tonight," he said, with the faintest hint of a leer, raising his eyebrows at Heck. "DO YOU SEE THAT, MOTHER! SHE MUST BE HAVING A . . ."

"SHU . . . SHU . . . SHUT UP!"

Lila Mae froze halfway to the door, and turned slowly around to the shocked tableau of Elmer and Heck, eyes popping.

"You . . . you . . . you d . . . don't haf . . . have to sh . . . shout," Mrs. Wallerby said slowly. Then she looked at Lila Mae, a beatific expression of satisfaction on her face, "You . . . you . . . ha . . . have a n . . . nice t . . . time, dear."

She had told Wellesley seven-thirty, hoping by that time the heat would have broken. Too, it gave her time for a soak in the tub, a little nap, and the complicated process Mrs. Rudolph had outlined for her the night before.

"Take the time that it takes," she had said. "If you're not satisfied, redo it. You should feel as beautiful as you want to when you're done."

Wellesley took a step back and whistled when he saw her, and rather than dismiss it, or belittle herself, she simply smiled. She did look nice. She had worked to look nice. There was no reason to pretend otherwise.

After dinner, in the early summer twilight, they drove for a while, and talked about old times at South Mockdon High, about all that had happened since then; about Wellesley's time in the service, which she had never heard about, and her time with Eddie. Too, she filled him in on the details of the "World of Love" scandal and how she had broken her television.

"You what?" he said incredulously.

"Put the telephone table right through it." She giggled. "And I'm proud of it."

He shook his head admiringly. "Well, I guess maybe Jackie's right. You are some kind of wildcat."

"I'll take that as a compliment," she said.

"Just exactly the way I meant it." He reached over and put his arm around her. "Just exactly."

Finally, though, it was late, and they both had to work next day. He turned slowly onto Zunis. For the last few blocks, they had not spoken. He pulled up in front of the duplex and cut the engine.

She rested her head on his shoulder, and they sat there a minute, cuddled together, warm and unspeaking. Then he leaned around and began to kiss her along her hairline, her cheekbones, snuggling her ears. Finally, as she felt his lips on hers, she slipped her hand to the back of his head and kissed him deeply on the mouth.

"Lila Mae, I . . ."

"Shhh," she said, trembling slightly. "Why don't you come in for a minute, Wellesley."

He seemed to hesitate. "But, Lila Mae, you've got to be up tomorrow, and I don't want . . . I mean, I wouldn't want to do something . . ."

She shushed him again and opened her door. He slid out on her side, and they went in the house.

When they first entered, he laughed at the blind eye of the television, still sitting against the far wall. She poured them both some iced tea, and they talked for a few minutes more before she reached for his hand. There on the sofa, in the quiet of her little house in the soft summer darkness, she felt his arms around her, and his lips against hers, as her hands touched his back, his chest, grasped that lean rump she had kicked so resoundingly in what now seemed another life. It was late and silent, lazy and warm. His breath tickled her neck, and throughout her whole self she felt a hot shudder uncoiling.

He pulled back suddenly.

"Lila Mae. Lila Mae, I think I better . . ." He stood up, rearranging his jeans. "I mean, I don't think I . . ."

She raised herself on one arm and touched his lips with her fingers. She reached for her purse, and, with nothing but touch to guide her in the black, pushed her billfold aside, her compact, a notepad, and another role of tape she had swiped. She found the box and pulled it out and pressed it into his hand.

Later, Wellesley would always laugh when she told the story. The story of that breakneck ride down the highway to North Mockdon, almost to the county line, that night she put a table through Ted Standish's face and threatened to wring her mother's neck. All the way to the Speedy Shop, where some lonely teenaged boy rang up her loaf of bread, bottle of Nehi, can of Campbell's pork and beans, Wrigley's Spearmint gum, and a box of Trojans. She had given him a ten-dollar bill and been so flustered she forgot to pick up her change and he'd chased her into the parking lot like the last avenging emissary of Ted and Becky to give her those three ones and a quarter. . . .

But that was later. That night, when it was done, when he lay beside her on the bed, dreamy and sated, his hand cradling her breast, both of them grinning, lazy as sleepy children, when he said to her, "Lila Mae, Lila Mae, how was it that you had these with you tonight?" she had simply smiled mysteriously.

Only when his breathing had slowed, and his eyes closed, and his whole body fell relaxed against hers, did she lean over to his tonic-sweet head and whisper in his ear, "Because, Wellesley Coe, one thing I've learned lately is that, in this life, you never want to have to regret that you never swam naked at the Taj Mahal."

EPILOGUE

It rained the next week, and the year that followed was one of the wetter ones in Mockdon County, at least to Lila Mae's best recollection. In the spring, there was a little flooding down near Olinda, but for the most part it was a gentle time, short and sudden thunderstorms in August, somber showers in late October, three or four whispering snowfalls in January and February, the April downpours to assure the blooms of May and June.

Standing there in the park next to the Episcopal church that Saturday afternoon, Lila Mae smiled out over the milling throng with their champagne or fruit punch, colorful on the deep, shady green of the lawn, the old quarry a sudden void in the distance. It was ironic, perhaps, that it was Eddie's family's church, but it was the closest to Macaffey's, where everything had started over again, and too it gave to all that had happened a certain aura of continuity, of tolerance.

She took Wellesley's newly beringed hand in her own, which sparkled once again with a simple gold band. Off to one side, Jackie Pomeroy had gathered a few other good old boys around with his guitar and they were singing songs that might not be entirely appropriate for a wedding reception, though, then again, it was perhaps the kind of naughty intimacy that marriage was supposed to finally give public voice to. If some of the words still made her blush a bit, she could look over at Wellesley's grin—amused, with just a hint too of embarrassment—and feel the sweet warmth of sharing, of accepting the tribute of friends, who, whether their choices were the best or not, tried to make this celebration one not only you but everybody in attendance would remember.

It had not been a completely straight road to the altar. It was not like it had been with Eddie, the logical procession from "Pomp and Circumstance" to "Here Comes the Bride." Wellesley Coe had been set for years in his bachelor ways, and Lila Mae herself, burned once and badly in romance, was twice wary of entanglements that might leave her lifeless as some ghostly lightning-blasted tree. After that first night of love, there had been a certain caution, a gradual getting-to-know that was determined to see past the light of passion, powerful but fickle, toward the softer, warmer glow of affection essential to sustain two people across years when lankiness or pertness has given way to the creaks and sags that, at Quiet Meadows, Lila Mae had come intimately to know.

She had not forgotten those old people she had learned to cherish, despite their demands and their crankiness and the small disasters they visited upon her day to day. Across the lawn, she spotted Mrs. Wallerby in her wheelchair, Elmer and Heck attending, fat as ever but soft-spoken in the last year. True to Eliot's prediction, her stutter had begun to fade. Nearby was Frank Meachum, still speechless but, especially today, a dervish of gestures and cockatoo of whistles in all the excitement. And Alice Fitzer in her wheelchair, chatting with Mrs. Lindley, who as usual had the strained look of someone certain that, instant to instant, something was bound to go wrong.

Mr. Ricks had died in March. Lila Mae, despite his doubts, had visited him now and then over the course of his slow departure. They had laughed about the time Frank Meachum brought the closet crashing down, and she had told him how she had never forgotten the story that he told her then, when her world seemed to be in about the same condition. After Christmas, he deteriorated rapidly, and was finally in the hospital at the end. She saw him three days before the final crisis. He was heavily medicated, but still peculiarly alert, and he promised her he still intended to take up a number of matters with God when he got settled in upstairs.

Lila Mae drifted down through the crowd, as Wellesley went to suggest to the Midas bunch that the songs might be getting a little too blue. She waved at Priscilla, there with some new man, who, Lila Mae had noted, drove a Dodge—a Dodge truck, it was true, but a Dodge nonetheless. Billie Jean had all her children in tow, and Lila Mae thought it was better than having a video camera, for, years and years from now, she could consult not only the wedding photographs but Billie Jean's memory to recall what was said and who talked with whom and at exactly what point in the ceremony it was that Alice had begun to cry because it was all too beautiful.

It was toward Norma and the others from Quiet Meadows

she was headed. Eliot had arrived on his bike in a leather vest and jeans, with Stewart on the back, dramatic in a white outfit that made him look like the president of one of those African countries that, in twenty years, she still had trouble keeping straight. Their friend Anita, with her friend Evie, had come as well, along with the head of the women's group that Norma had belonged to for a while. They were all standing together, Norma's arm around Murray, a professor of psychology down in the capital. In January, Norma had moved, the direction of her desires still undecided, and started back to school. She had begun to date Murray two months before, but it was, she made clear to Lila Mae, still very much an open relationship, for she could not truly commit herself to anyone else, man or woman, till she truly understood herself. Lila Mae feared that process might test the patience of anyone, regardless of gender.

"Well, Lila Mae," Stewart said, "now that you're a married lady again, are we going to be losing you?"

She smiled. "Not till the babies come, Stewart. I'd go crazy being a homebody till then, and I don't plan to have to depend on Midas Muffler to get us what we want."

Eliot was wearing a bulky silver necklace that looked like nothing so much as a dog's choke chain.

"Why, Eliot," she said, scrutinizing it, "what an interesting piece."

She noticed Stewart had his hand stuck in the back pocket of Eliot's jeans. "It's my turn to wear it this month." He smirked. "And that's all you want to know about it, Lila Mae."

She shook her head, and chatted for a minute with Anita and Evie. She was still not sure she understood these people, but she did know, after a year at Quiet Meadows, that their loves and losses were as real as anybody else's, and that, if it came down to a battle between the Teds and Beckys of the world versus the Stewarts and Eliots, there was no question of where her loyalties would lie.

Momma was deep in conversation with Mrs. Rudolph and Wellesley's mother, showing off her crystals, which to Lila Mae's mind, regardless of her new openness, were occult. But Momma had seen a former Pentecostal on UHF who gave Scriptural justification for their special powers, and Lila Mae was not about to get into an argument about it. Certainly, Momma, like everybody else, would have more than enough to answer for at the Celestial Bench without questions about faddish superstitions coming up. Lonnie and Betsy were there beside her with Cindy; Billy and Diana were picking at each other just beyond their parents' view.

She sidled up to her brothers, who were chatting with Wellesley's three: Tully, Stan, and Obie. Lonnie was busy trying to convince the first to invest in the remodeling of the old Ford dealership downtown, while the two others listened to Little Joey extol the virtues of Oregon, to which, he told Lila Mae the night he arrived, he was returning as soon as she and Wellesley left for their honeymoon. Fred stood a little aside, taking it all in.

She hooked her arm in his. "So when will we be doing this for you?"

He grinned sadly. "Oh, it'll be a while, Lila Mae. I figure it'll take all my energy to keep Momma off your and Wellesley's tails for the first few years. Nothing wrecks a marriage easier than kin."

He was right, of course, for even though, since that night with Monkra in the family living room, things had definitely changed, Momma still took up a fair amount of her free time,

time she now intended to spend on her marriage, thank you. And Fred would do as he said—good-hearted, half-drunk, and alone—till Momma departed. Unless, and it pained Lila Mae to think it as she hugged him, he ended up going first.

Standing slightly apart were Eddie and Mary Gonzalez, who was now far enough along to be showing it. Sammy Stephens was beside them, his hand on Mary's shoulder. He had already had a bit too much champagne, but had warned Lila Mae he intended to overindulge.

"It's only right," he told her, "that I celebrate a bit. I mean, I was the one, legally, who put you two asunder. So, I get to whoop it up when each of you's finally joined together again, even if it's with someone else, right?"

Lila Mae had not gone to their wedding. At the time, not so long after she'd taken up again with Wellesley, it had seemed early. But now, with her own life set on a new course, she could welcome them both, and feel a hint of sadness only at how she and Eddie had misread themselves and what they needed in those years before. Still, she let herself remember only the best of things with him, the first years, when their love was fresh in the way it can perhaps only be the first time around, when it is wonderful, though not wise.

And wise, she thought serenely, turning around to see her husband with Jackie at his side, was what she had now. A wise love with a good man who cherished her purely and deeply and simply, with whom she might make a life and raise a family. Times might change, of course. In the future, they might feel differently. But that would have to be dealt with then, and, on this day, she felt no fear of phantom shadows of the still-to-come.

By this time, Lila Mae had reached the steps of the church,

and she climbed up to stand on the porch so she could look out over them all: Momma and her brothers; Norma and Priscilla and Billie Jean; Frank Meachum, Alice Fitzer, and Mrs. Wallerby; Stewart and Eliot; Eddie and Mary; Sammy Stephens and all the rest. And it occurred to her then that, perhaps, Ted and Becky had had a certain point, that it was a world of love, though not in the neat and constricted way they had imagined it. Rather than a certain and rulebound place, it was a world in which all was random, spontaneous, in constant flux, and you could make terrible, terrible mistakes, ones you could not correct, ones that, as Mr. Ricks had told you, you would always regret. Then all you could do was move forward, and accept what was given to you. But sometimes there were extraordinary surprises in store, and, in the end, you did not have to be Richard Halliburton, wandering across half the world, to know the pages of the *Book of Marvels*. And perhaps, she thought, if you were kind and good and tried to love the best you knew how, you might feel some certainty as well that your name was recorded in the Book of Life.

She surveyed them all again: Motley and crazy and cranky and queer.

Despite it all, she thought Jesus would approve.